BELLYACHE

A Delicious Tale

by
CRYSTAL MARCOS

Cat Marcs Publishing
Silverdale, Washington

Cat Marcs Publishing
PO Box 54
Silverdale, WA 98383

www.CatMarcs.com

Printed in the United States of America

ISBN 978-0-9843899-0-2
LCCN 2009913303

For my "sweet" family and all God's creatures, great and small.

Contents

BELLYACHE

Helping Papa

It was a school holiday and Peter Fischer had to spend the day working with his grandfather. His parents had jobs and Peter, now ten, felt he was too old for a babysitter. He had never been to work with Papa before. His grandfather owned a sweet shop. Papa's Sweet Shop. Peter was excited. What fun he would have tasting all the luscious treats!

Peter planned his day in his head. First, a cupcake with heaps of whipped cream icing. Then, several pieces of chocolate filled with all kinds of wonderful centers. Next, red licorice. He thought black licorice tasted gross; he only knew one person who liked it and that was old man Rupert. Old man Rupert lived a few houses down and was always in the garden, fiddling around with a piece of black licorice dangling out of the corner of his mouth—disgusting.

After lunch, a peppermint, followed by a chocolate chip cookie, half a brownie—he wanted to save room for other sweets—Tootsie Rolls, and lemon drops. Then, he would take a break from eating and help Papa with the afternoon rush of customers. After the rush, a few gumdrops and gumballs—the blue ones of course—and then gooey taffy, followed by gummy bears and super sour gummy worms. Lastly, he would have his most favorite treat of all, creamy chocolaty peanut butter cups—two or three of them, he wasn't quite sure yet.

But Papa had a different plan for Peter.

"Hello, Peter. I am so glad to have you as my little helper today. As a reward for your work, you may have three pieces of candy." Papa grinned. "Go on now, pick out what you want and put them in the back for later."

"Just three?" Peter moped.

"I think three is plenty. We don't want you to get cavities or make yourself sick." Papa smiled and pushed his glasses back on the bridge of his nose. "Now go on, pick."

Just three, Peter thought to himself. What about all that planning he had done? Well, he would have to think about his choices ever so carefully. Peter took a small plastic plate down from the counter, already knowing one of his choices. He needed to pick the other two. He opened the case to the heavenly chocolates and was nearly knocked off his feet by the grand smells of the freshly made candies. How could he pick just three? He made his first choice, a milk chocolate chunk. He made his second choice, dark-chocolate-covered nougat. He was about to put his last choice, his creamy chocolaty peanut butter cup, onto his plate when he noticed Papa was busy with a customer. He grabbed another peanut butter cup and turned quickly to go to the back room. He put his plate down on the little table next to the picture of Papa and Nana on the wall. He turned around so he wasn't facing the picture, and devoured the extra peanut butter cup before returning to the front to help Papa.

Papa asked, "Are you happy with your choices, Peter?"

"Oh yes, thank you, Papa."

"Good, now help me stock the gummy jars before the afternoon rush. Go and get the gummies in the back room," Papa ordered.

Peter saw the gummies stacked on a red wagon. He started to roll them to the front of the store when he thought he would have a couple super sour gummy worms and a few gummy bears. No one would ever know the difference. Peter gobbled them up on the way to the front. They were so yummy, and the worms were almost too sour, he was afraid Papa would see his scrunched-up face. But Papa didn't. Peter stocked the gummies and helped Papa with a few customers.

One was an incredibly tall woman with bright red hair and a sharp jaw.

"Peter, come here." Papa said. "I want you to meet Mrs. Nielson. She has been a customer of mine since the day we opened, and she comes in every Monday for a special batch of fudge. Go and fetch it in the refrigerator, please."

"Hello, nice to meet you," Peter said.

The woman smiled back.

Peter looked in the huge walk-in refrigerator and saw a white box labeled "Mrs. Nielson." He took the box, and right behind it, staring back at him, was more fudge, lots and lots of fudge, stacked high. Surely Papa would not miss just one piece. So he stuffed one in his mouth and swallowed as quickly as possible, almost so fast he couldn't taste it. On the way to the front, he grabbed one of his own candies off of his plate on the table. It was the milk chocolate chunk, and it was terrific!

When he saw his grandfather, Peter was still chewing the last bit of his chunk. "I had one of my candies. That's okay, right?"

"Of course, Peter, you deserve it." Papa grinned, taking Mrs. Nielsen's fudge from Peter.

Peter watched the door as she left and saw the postman coming in. He was a short man with thick black hair and glasses like Papa's. He handed Papa a few letters and a medium-sized box marked "Special Delivery" in bright red.

Wonder what's in there? Peter thought.

"Would you like a caramel for the road, Lucian?" Papa asked.

"You know I would!" admitted Lucian. "And who is this young fellow?"

"This is my grandson, Peter. He is helping me out around the store today," Papa said proudly.

"You must be having a good time," Lucian said, biting into his caramel. Caramel dripped from his mouth, and he licked his lips to make sure he got every last morsel.

"Yes, sir," Peter answered.

"When your grandfather and I were little, we hardly ever got any candy. You are a very fortunate boy to have a grandfather who owns a sweet shop. Well, I'd love to stay, but I must be on my way."

Peter thought about what Lucian had said. It was true; he was a fortunate boy. When Peter was younger, Papa told him a story about when he was a boy in Germany and his family did not have much money. A generous neighbor used to put pennies in a tree in their backyard and tell him and his brothers to shake it. The neighbor called it a magic tree. When they shook the magic tree, the pennies fell out and scattered around like copper treasures. It brought the neighbor great joy to see their faces light up. Papa and his brothers would gather up the coins and run straight to the general store to buy some candy. He tried to make his candy last as long as possible, doing things like licking a piece of candy one long stroke at a time instead of sticking the whole thing in his mouth. Now he had a candy shop of his very own.

The phone rang and brought Peter back to reality. He heard Papa talking but he wasn't really listening.

Papa hung up and told Peter to open the bottom drawer near the cupcakes and get out six candies that said "Happy Birthday" on them and put them on six chocolate cupcakes with vanilla frosting.

Papa said he would put them in a box when he came back from using the bathroom. He was sure Peter could cover the store for a few minutes.

Once Peter was alone, he did as his papa asked. The smell of the mixture of the vanilla and chocolate was too much for him to handle. How fast could he eat a cupcake? He looked at the shelf lined with cupcakes and took one. Peter definitely could eat one fast because it was gone before he knew it, and Papa was not back yet. He shoved the cupcake paper into the front pocket of his cargo shorts.

At that moment, Papa appeared with a box for the cupcakes. He even had purple and red ribbon to tie it with.

"I need you to take these down to Ruthie's Carpets." Papa reached into the penny dish. "Make sure you give them this when they give you the money." He handed him a penny.

Inside Ruthie's, a small bundle of fluff greeted him at the door and he nearly dropped the cupcakes from surprise. It was a dog who was sniffing Peter's shoe. A woman with peppered white hair called the dog over and waved Peter in. The woman's name tag said "Ruthie."

"Hello, I have your cupcakes."

"Thank you very much. Joyce has been trying to keep her birthday a secret from us, but we found out and couldn't let it pass by without doing anything," Ruthie said.

Suddenly, there were four other people beside

him. One man said, laughing, "We smelled those cupcakes and came runnin'!"

"I am going to pass on the cupcake," a robust man said, patting his stomach. "I promised my doctor I would watch what I eat."

He turned to Peter and asked, "Hey, kid, do you want mine?"

Peter looked at Ruthie for approval.

"If it doesn't spoil your lunch, I don't see why not," she answered.

"No, it won't," said Peter.

They sang "Happy Birthday" to Joyce and ate the cupcakes. Peter was right; they loved them. Ruthie gave Peter the money, and he made sure to give her the penny before he headed back to Papa. On his way back, he felt a little grumble in his stomach. He knew that feeling...he was starting to get full. He thought to himself he would lay off of eating anything for a while. Another grumble.

Lunch Time

When Peter arrived at the store, he heard a familiar song. As soon as the off-key notes hit his ears, he knew who was there. Nana!

Peter watched Papa bending down to pick a piece of trash off the floor to throw it away. Papa pushed his glasses back up on his nose again when he turned to face Peter. Peter thought Papa really should tape those things to his ears. It may look a little funny but at least he wouldn't have to keep fixing them all day.

"I hear Nana's song." Peter smiled.

Papa chuckled. "Yes, she is in the back. She has brought us a nice lunch."

"Lunch?" Peter thought he might get sick. Hopefully it would be for much later.

Peter handed his grandfather the money for the birthday cupcakes and found Nana in the back room, unpacking a large blue carrying case.

Oh no! Peter's head screamed. *I'll just tell her I am not hungry. No, I can't. She might catch on. I could still have room to eat...not a lot of room.*

"Peter, come over here and give me a hug. I missed you!" Nana shrieked with joy.

Nana always said she missed him even though

she had seen him just two days earlier. Peter wrapped his arms around his grandmother. He still couldn't touch his hands together. He figured one day his arms would be long enough to do that.

"I have made lunch for us all: turkey sandwiches with cranberry sauce, carrot sticks, and milk." Nana beamed.

Peter smiled back and said, "Thanks, Nana," even though he wished she hadn't brought anything.

"Now go and wash up so we can eat," she ordered.

Peter stood there for a moment. How could he eat all that? He knew he would have to because Nana always made him clean his plate. She would say that a growing boy needs his energy.

Papa interrupted his thoughts when he stuck his head in the doorway.

"Peter, you have a visitor. Come and see who it is."

"A visitor?" Peter wondered who it was.

At any rate, he did not really care as long as he did not have to eat right now.

When Peter arrived at the front, he saw a blond man. He did not recognize him. He did not see anyone else. Then Papa moved a little to the right and he saw his visitor. It was Lina Young. He was happy to see her. He really liked Lina because she wasn't a girly girl. They would hang out at recess sometimes and talk mostly about baseball and other sports if they weren't playing them.

Lina was pretty tough, too. One time they were sitting on a bench and looking at one of her dad's sports magazines. An older kid, Harmon, came over and bellowed, "What are you girls looking at? Probably a ladies' magazine! Hey, Peter, why are you hanging out with a girl, and one who is Asian anyway!"

Hearing that made Peter mad, but before he had a chance to react, Lina had Harmon in a head-lock and was shoving the magazine in his face, pointing out, "I don't read sissy magazines, and even if I did, it is none of your business! What makes me different is what makes me special!" It was funny to see a petite girl holding an older, much taller kid in a headlock. Harmon never bugged them again.

"Hi, Peter. So this is what you are doing on your day off. Cool." Lina nodded in approval.

Peter saw the blond man moving closer, and he stopped right next to Lina.

"Dad, this is Peter, my friend. Peter, this is my dad," she said, gesturing to them both. They exchanged hellos.

She must have seen the confusion on Peter's face. "My mom is Filipino," she informed him.

Peter nodded in acknowledgement.

"My dad said I could get some stuff that has to last all week. Wanna help me?"

Peter helped Lina pick out a variety of treats while Papa and Mr. Young chatted. Peter made sure to take his time with Lina. Every minute meant he did not have to eat Nana's lunch. He found out Lina's favorite sweet shop treat was the Jelly Belly Prehistoric Dinosaur Egg. Peter agreed that they were pretty good, with the speckled outer shell formed into an egg filled with milk chocolate, and the cool surprise inside: a dinosaur-shaped fruit snack candy.

He also found out that Lina did not care for gum. She said she hadn't chewed the stuff since she was six years old and she fell asleep with a large wad in her mouth and it ended up in her hair and left eyebrow. Her parents had to cut her hair into a bob to get all the gum out and would have had to shave her eyebrow too if the peanut butter they rubbed on it hadn't worked. That is when she decided to keep her hair shorter because it was faster to get ready for school in the morning and easier to play sports.

Lina made sure to get her mother a slice of dark chocolate fudge. She said, "My dad and I wouldn't touch this; we aren't dark chocolate fans." She stuck her tongue out in disgust.

"I don't mind it," Peter said.

Lina grimaced.

After they gathered up what they decided was a good stash of sweets, her dad paid, and Peter and his Papa watched them leave. Peter thought that he wasn't any less hungry.

Papa looked at his watch and said, "Time for lunch." He walked to the front door and turned the sign over and moved the red hands of the clock to say, "Be back at 12:30 p.m."

Shoot, Peter thought.

Nana sat at the neatly set lunch table, knitting something that he was pretty sure was a hat of some kind.

"What are you knitting?" Peter asked her.

"A cap for your new baby cousin, just like the one I made for you when you were a baby," Nana replied, patting Peter on his head.

He was sick of hearing about the baby this and the baby that. Up until now, Peter had been the youngest grandchild, and it had been pretty cozy. He did not think the baby was all that great, anyway. He had no hair and looked purple and shriveled. Prune Baby.

Peter took his time washing his hands and getting seated at the table, where he fidgeted for a while before starting to eat. The sandwich wasn't as tasty as usual, not because of Nana's sandwich-making skills but because nothing tastes as good if you are not hungry. Towards the end of lunch, Peter's cargo shorts began to get tight around the waist, and he was starting to feel bloated. As usual, Nana made sure he cleared his plate. He did not think he could finish the last bite. He tried to leave it on his plate, when Nana gave him the look that meant, "Finish up eating." He reluctantly chewed and swallowed it. *Thank goodness I am done*, Peter thought. Nana got up and went to the front and quickly returned. She had a chocolate chip cookie in each hand.

"Papa and I decided since you were such a good helper today that you could have a cookie for dessert," Nana said, handing Peter a cookie.

Peter took it even though he did not want it.

"Thank you," Peter almost whispered. He stared at it and thought maybe if he stared at it hard enough, it would disappear. When he looked up, Nana and Papa had almost finished their cookies. Nana smiled back at Peter. There was chocolate on her front tooth. Peter's stomach churned. He knew he had to eat the cookie or they might suspect something. He never turned down sweets from Papa or Nana, ever. Maybe they would get up before he was done and he could hide the cookie in his shoe or flush it down the toilet. No such luck. Peter ate small bites in between talking and kept thinking that when his stomach could no longer be controlled by his cargo shorts, the button was going to pop off and hit Nana right in the middle of her forehead. He almost giggled at the thought.

Finally, he was done. No more eating until dinner or maybe not even then. He felt sick, sick like the time he saw Curtis Wheeler throw up in the cafeteria all over Hanna Dell.

"Are you all right, Peter?" Papa looked concerned.

Peter quickly answered, "Yes, I have to burp." It sounded as good as anything.

"All right then, let's get back to work," Papa

ordered.

Peter slowly got up and went to the front to say good-bye to Nana.

"I will miss you so much." Nana kissed him on his forehead. "I will be counting down the days till I see your smiling face in church on Sunday." He watched her turn the sign over to say "Open" on the way out the door. He wished he was going with her to lie on her cushy floral couch, which swallowed him with comfort every time he visited. That would make him feel better. Why did he have to eat all those sweets? He thought about how he should have paced himself or said, "Yes, it would spoil my lunch," to Ruthie the carpet lady. He thought about the time: five more hours until Papa took him home. Would he be able to handle it?

Papa's voice interrupted his thoughts. "I need you to try something for me."

"Try something?" Peter's voice had no enthu-siasm.

"A new candy I have made," Papa reported. "I haven't put it out for sale yet because I was going to present it to your Nana first for our anniversary. It is a chocolate-covered dried mango slice with coconut sprinkled on top. You know how Nana loves exotic flavors. She should really enjoy this. Try it and tell me how you like it." Papa opened a tissue paper to display the new candy.

Peter's mind went in two different directions. *What a great thing Papa has done for Nana! There is no way I could eat anything else right now!*

He heard the door behind him open and saw the new candy disappearing once again into the tissue paper. Saved again by customers!

Sweetness Overload

Peter swung around and greeted the customers with the enthusiasm he lacked earlier. "Hello, how may I help you today? We have lots of exceptional stuff to choose from." Peter realized he probably sounded like a dork. But he did not care. Anything to keep him from eating. The two ladies smiled back and seemed to be amused by Peter's peppy attitude. Right behind them, a young man and a young woman entered. More customers! Peter made sure to talk to each person to prolong their stay. The longer they stayed, the longer until he ate. He did not feel well, but he could not show it. He was not going to disappoint Papa and let him know he had been sneaking sweets. Business stayed steady for a while, customers coming and going and Peter chatting. Finally, it died down.

Peter had hoped that Papa would forget about the tissue with Nana's anniversary surprise. He still did not feel well, and all that talking had made him feel heavier. His stomach let out a loud, long growl. He looked at the red and yellow tiles on the floor and thought about lying down on them. But he knew he couldn't.

"Here, Peter, come and taste," said Papa

briskly.

Oh spam! he thought. He used this term when he wanted to say something he wasn't supposed to. He said it once when he stubbed his toe on the coffee table at home, and his mother did not seem to mind. Ever since then, a few people had caught on to using the term. Even his mother said it sometimes when she opened bills or couldn't find a parking spot at the mall.

Peter took the candy. He studied it while Papa watched. *Better eat it quickly to get it over with,* he told himself. The candy did not have a fighting chance for Peter to like it—not because it wasn't good, but because Peter would never want to think about it or eat it again. It was going to be too much for him to handle. It was going to be the one thing that pushed him over the edge, the one thing that would send him to the bathroom.

Peter managed to get out, "It is very good, Papa. Nana will really appreciate it."

"Thank you." Papa's smile quickly turned into a grimace. "Peter, are you feeling well? You look a little green."

Peter clutched his stomach. "I think I have to go to the bathroom." He quickly took off towards the back room. He was missing for quite some time. Unfortunately, he still felt horrible. His stomach kept bubbling, and all he wanted to do was lie down!

"Peter, are you sick?" Papa asked, concerned.

"No, I am fine," Peter mustered.

Papa responded, "Well, you don't look so good. Sit down and see if you feel better after a while."

Peter did as he was told. Papa put his hand to Peter's head. "You don't seem to have a fever. Maybe Papa's working you too hard?"

Peter wasn't going to confess to being a glutton. He did not want Papa to know what he had been up to. Aside from eating all that junk, he rather enjoyed working at Papa's Sweet Shop and he did not want to mess up the chance of ever being able to again.

Peter answered, "No, you are not working me too hard. I am having fun." *Fun minus the sick feeling*, he reminded himself.

"At any rate, Peter, you sit down and rest, and I will check on you later," insisted Papa.

Peter agreed to rest. He took the seats Papa and Nana usually sat on and put them on the side of the wall near Nana's photo. He saw the two candies he had picked out this morning staring at him, and he grabbed a paper towel to hide them from his sight. *What a dummy I have been, sneaking all those things. I never want to eat sweets again. Not until next week, anyway,* he told himself as he plopped himself onto his makeshift bed.

Staying up late last night was taking its toll. Not feeling well didn't help matters either. His eyes were starting to droop, droop, droop, droop, and every once in a while, he heard his stomach make foreign noises. Soon, he was asleep.

Left Behind

A loud thud startled Peter awake. He quickly sat up and was shocked to find it dark, with the exception of a few dim lights from the equipment Papa used to make his goodies and a gleam of light under the doorway.

What is going on? He pushed the button on his watch that made the face glow. It was 5:42 p.m. Had Papa gone home and forgotten him? Papa had been known to forget things sometimes.

Then he noticed a package in the spot where he had left his candies. Was that what had woken him up?

A sense of calm swept over Peter. Papa must not be very far since he just put the package on the table. He ran to the front of the store. There were no lights on there, either. It was getting dark outside. No sign of Papa!

Peter remembered he had not checked the bathroom. Maybe Papa was in there. There was still hope that he hadn't been left behind. He hurried to the back and went straight to the door, calling out to Papa on his way there. He looked beneath the bathroom door to see if he could see any light coming out. No light. He opened the door.

Peter was taken aback to see someone staring at him in the dark. He jumped back and let go of the door. Then he realized it was his own reflection in the mirror. He laughed at himself. Peter had scared himself like this once before when he looked out the kitchen sliding glass door.

The refrigerator! He thought maybe Papa was stocking it. He swung it open and found only food.

Then he came to the realization that Papa had forgotten him. Maybe Papa could not see him behind the table and had gotten so busy he forgot about him.

"This stinks," he admitted out loud.

He wasn't sure if he should wait for a few minutes in case Papa remembered him or if he should call his mother. He did not want Papa to get a lecture about being forgetful. He decided to wait five minutes. Then he would call his mother. There was no sense waiting in the dark, so Peter ventured to find the light switch. He thought he would pass time by pretending he was a pirate searching for buried treasure in a dark cave, and he needed one of those torches that pirates light on fire in the movies.

He was beginning to enjoy himself when he heard an unfamiliar humming sound. The humming was getting louder every second. *What is that?* Peter was perplexed. It sounded as though it was coming from the area where Peter had made his makeshift bed. He remembered the package on the table; it was slightly opened. Had it been opened before? The red letters on the package, which read "Special Delivery," began to get brighter, glowing in the dark like a neon light with every hum. The words seemed to be popping off the box.

Oh spam! Peter thought. He was captivated by the beauty of the red glowing letters and could no longer hear the loud humming.

Standing over the package, Peter tried to peek inside, but he could not see anything. He was taken by surprise by a delightful warm gust of air blowing in his face from the box—the kind of breeze Peter had felt on many warm summer days.

He put his hands on the side flaps of the box and took a deep breath. He felt compelled to open it. He was astonished to see nothing inside—no bottom of the box, no table underneath. It was completely dark, a bottomless pit. Peter leaned in for a closer look. The next thing he knew, the box began stretching up toward the ceiling. Peter gasped and took a step back. The opening of the box leaned toward Peter as if to get a closer look at him. Peter could not move.

An overwhelming sense of peace swept over him, and he couldn't keep from cracking a little smile. As soon as the corners of his mouth turned upward, the package swallowed him whole and made a giant gulping noise!

Peter was not frightened, although he was surrounded by darkness. He seemed to be standing on a solid surface. Every few seconds, there was a tiny flicker of colorful light: first purple, then blue, then yellow, then pink, and many different colors followed. All of them were twinkling, like little stars in the darkness. Soon there were a small number of other colors flickering at the same time, faster and faster, more and more every second, until he was surrounded by thousands of the twinkling stars. Unexpectedly, they were no longer blinking, and it was as though he was encircled by a beautiful sea of lights giving off warmth.

Peter thought it was absolutely one of the coolest things he had ever seen. The events had momentarily made him forget about the earlier part of the day. It was very peaceful, and he finally noticed his belly no longer ached. Peter turned his attention back to the stars and wondered if he could touch them. Would they be too hot, like miniature light bulbs? He decided the only way to find out was to touch one. He focused his attention on a luminous green one directly across from his nose. "You're it," he said to the little fellow, half expecting to hear an echo. There was no echo.

Raising his finger directly toward the star, Peter hardly blinked. At the touch of Peter's finger, the little light went out. All the other lights kept shining, but there was a little black hole in the place where the green light had once shone so brightly. Peter swiftly returned his arm to his side and felt extremely guilty. Without warning, one by one, just as they had appeared, the colorful lights disappeared faster and faster, more and more, every second until there was darkness again. "Sorry!" Peter called out with true regret. But it was too late. The lights were gone, and he was alone.

Out of the darkness came a disturbing, ear-splitting rumbling noise, and the solid surface under him seemed to turn into gelatin, waving his body back and forth like a kite in the wind. Before Peter could think about what was happening, the gelatin sucked him down farther. The next thing he knew, he was being shot straight up into the blackness, leaving the gelatin far behind. The rumbling noise faded as he soared higher and higher.

Peter shut his eyes, wishing he had never touched that poor little green light. *What have I done? Where am I going?* Peter's body came to an abrupt stop. He opened his eyes. To his amazement, he was no longer encircled by the darkness.

Look at That!

Wherever Peter was, it was like no place he had ever seen before, not even on TV. He looked down at his feet and lifted up his sneakers to check if anything odd was stuck to them. He saw nothing unusual. He looked around for a warp hole like those he had seen in video games; there was nothing like that. He took a deep breath. There was a slight sweet scent to the air; he couldn't quite place the smell. It was warm, but not as warm as when he was surrounded by the twinkling lights.

Peter's eyes explored his new environment. He saw a few trees that looked like the ones in his backyard at home, only there was something different. The leaves were the same color as the grass, bluish-green, and their branches all seemed to be pointing in the same direction. *Toward what?* Peter wondered. He turned his attention to the sky. He was a little disappointed to see it was a normal-looking sky with a few clouds and the sun shining. Peter listened intently but could hear nothing except for the sounds of nature. He realized he was alone, alone in a strange place with bluish-green grass and pointing trees. No one to explore with, no one to talk to, no one to ask how to get home! Peter began to panic. His heart started beating more rapidly. He felt hot and sweaty all over. His eyes started to well up with tears. Peter wasn't going to cry; he would not let himself.

"You must be brave, Peter," he told himself sternly.

Peter recalled a story Papa had told him about a family camping trip he had taken as a boy. Papa had gone off by himself to collect wood for the fire and was awe-stricken when he saw a quirky squirrel running through the wilderness. Papa followed him for quite some time before he did not recognize his surroundings. He was lost for hours. Papa told of how he was fearless and found his way back in the twilight to his worried family, with firewood in hand. Peter thought Papa wouldn't be proud if he found out his grandson had been a sniveling baby.

Something smooth rubbed up against the back of Peter's right leg. It scared Peter so badly he jumped. His heart was beating faster than ever. He swung around to see what it was, even though he feared what it might be.

Peter could hardly believe his eyes. Standing in the midst of the grass was a wondrous red and white cat. Once Peter smelled the sweet scent of the creature, he knew at once what it must be.

"Look at that; a peppermint cat!" he marveled.

The unmistakable stripes, red and white. Its wide eyes shone deep blue, its nose rose-red, its mouth a softer red. Its whiskers were like a regular cat's. Only this was no ordinary cat. Its scent was sweet peppermint and its smooth body was perfectly round like a peppermint candy, with four little legs peeking out underneath. A silky tail sprouted out in the back.

Peter looked around once more to see if he could share this amazing sight with anyone. Still no one. Peter started to frown but stopped when he saw the peppermint cat plop down on its stomach and begin licking its paw. Peter was grinning from ear to ear now.

"I wonder if you taste like peppermint," Peter told the cat.

The peppermint cat looked up at Peter with an inviting look while continuing to lick its paw. Peter soon gently sat down next to the cat's side; he left two feet of grass between them. The cat licked its paw for a few more seconds and then got up and closed the gap of grass between them, practically sitting on Peter's lap.

"Do you want me to pet you?" Peter asked softly.

The cat didn't respond. It sat there, seeming to stare at one of the pointing trees. Peter, a little worried he might scare off the cat, lifted his left hand toward the brilliant creature. Slowly and gently, he began to stroke the cat. The cat felt smooth and sleek. Its tail was also smooth. Peter thought it felt like the surface of a marble. The cat started to purr. Peter began to relax as he watched the chest of the cat rise and fall with its every breath. He couldn't resist sniffing his hand to see if it smelled like peppermint. It didn't, and he felt silly for doing so. They sat together in silence for several minutes while Peter petted and the peppermint cat purred.

Peter was thinking how he might find his way home when the peppermint cat rose on all fours and pushed its hind side up in the air to stretch. The cat returned to a normal stance and began to walk off. Peter staggered to his feet.

"Where are you going?" he cried out to the cat.

The peppermint cat glanced back casually at Peter and continued on its way. The only thing Peter could think to do was to follow the cat. He did not want to be alone, wherever he was. Maybe there would be more peppermint cats where he was going. Peter observed they were going the way the trees seemed to be pointing. Each time he passed a tree, he walked faster. He felt as though the trees had some sort of authority over him.

At the fourth tree they had passed, Peter heard a chirping noise. *A bird,* he thought right away. *Another life form!* Peter paused momentarily to see if he could spot the bird. There it was, perched on a branch, as vibrant yellow as could be. Peter took a couple of cautious steps toward it; he did not want it to fly away. He examined the bird from where he stood and couldn't believe his eyes. It was a fluffy marshmallow bird! A gigantic version of the ones he received on Easter. Had he gone mad? A peppermint cat and now a marshmallow bird? He turned to face the peppermint cat to make sure it was still within view. It was. He returned to watch the bird. It had flown down to the base of the tree and began pecking at the dirt beneath the grass. Within a flash, it had caught something and was trying to get the wiggly worm in its beak. Peter took a closer look. Could that possibly be a gummy worm? Of course, it had to be! He leaned in for an even closer look, and the marshmallow bird flew off with its meal. Disappointed, Peter hurried to catch up with his red and white companion.

Peter was now approaching a hill. He watched the cat disappear over the crest, then stopped dead in his tracks as he heard a horn honk, a low whistle of cars passing, and the barely audible voices of what sounded like children at play in the distance. Excited, he started up the hill full speed only to freeze again. What if those noises weren't what he suspected them to be? What if those noises were connected to things not as welcoming as the peppermint cat?

"Peter, you have got to be brave. Toughen up, pal," he said to himself forcefully. "How will you ever know what is over that hill if you don't look?"

Peter moved to the top of the hill, encouraging himself along the way. Papa would be proud. When he reached the top, he felt triumphant. The air was sweeter here.

What stood before him was spectacular: a

town of extraordinary-looking houses painted in bright, vivid colors. It reminded him of the gumball machine in Papa's Sweet Shop. The houses shone glossy in the sunlight. He supposed his mother would probably gasp at the sight. She would never dream of painting their house like any of these houses. Not Peter. He thought it was neat. They were all different shapes and sizes: rectangles, triangles, pentagons, hexagons, squares, and even a few circles. He could not see any peppermint cats or marshmallow birds. As a matter of fact, from where he was positioned, he could not see any living beings. He would have to venture into the town.

By now he was feeling pretty confident as he strutted forward. He passed tulips lining the side of an apple green triangle house. As he rounded the corner of the house, he was knocked backward a few steps by a yellow blur with a strong lemony scent. When Peter could focus his eyes, he fixed them on a radiant yellow...*boy?* Peter's lower jaw dropped fast. He was stunned.

Rude and Otherwise

The yellow boy disapproved of Peter's expression and said, "Don't you know it is rude to stare at someone that way? Didn't your parents teach you any manners? You humans are all the same." The boy crossed his arms.

Peter was amazed. It talked! He did, however, manage to lift his jaw back up and soften his face. "Sorry, I didn't mean to offend you. I have never seen anything like you before."

Agitated, the boy said, "I am not an 'anything'; I am a Candonite boy of the lemon drop race, and proud of it. And don't you dare even think of taking a bite out of me!"

Peter examined the Candonite closer. Yes, he saw it now: the pointed top and bottom of his body and round center were covered in sugary skin. A giant talking lemon drop with arms and legs!

"I wouldn't do that," Peter assured him.

"Now if you are done with your staring, you better come with me. My name is Joe, by the way."

"Joe." Peter let out a partial laugh before stopping himself.

"What? Is my name somehow funny to you?"

"No," said Peter. "I...didn't expect you to say

Joe."

"Oh," Joe said slyly. "Did you expect me to say Lemony, Yellowy, or maybe Zesty?

"I am very sorry. Joe is a nice name. My name is Peter," Peter said sincerely.

"Come with me," Joe snapped, walking away.

Peter obediently followed. He figured at least he was with someone who knew his way around.

"Where we are going isn't far from here, and I suspect you're going to want to ask me a million questions until we get there. But you can save them for when we get there," Joe demanded.

"Where is 'there'?" asked Peter.

"I said save your questions for when we get there," huffed Joe.

Peter did have lots of questions. *What town was it?* he wondered. But he would have to save that question for when he got to wherever they were going. There were mailboxes, all miniature versions of their respective houses. The trees here weren't pointing any particular way. The streets were not dark gray asphalt like the ones back home. They were glittery like candy wrappers—long, giant, multi-colored candy wrappers. There weren't any white lines in the middle. How did they know what side of the street to drive on? They passed a perfectly round, plum purple house. Roped to a tree in its front yard was what Peter thought must have been a dog, because it barked as they walked by. It looked just like a Tootsie Roll with short stubby legs. So as not to bother Joe, he waved at the Tootsie dog and gave it a wide smile.

The sound of a car engine from behind them caused Peter's head to snap in its direction. Peter saw immediately that the car had no tires. It glided a foot above the road. He noticed that it was gold and said "Police" on the side. It stopped across from them. The windows were so dark he couldn't see inside. Peter gulped. He had heard from kids at school that you never want the police to stop for you. Joe had turned to look at the car but did not seem as concerned as Peter.

The driver's-side window of the car slowly came down and revealed a skinny red Candonite with a dark brown handlebar mustache.

"Hello, Joe, I see you have yourself a human there. You boys better jump in the car. I'll get you to your destination quicker." The police officer spoke like Mr. Angus, a friend of Peter's father who was from Scotland. The Candonite officer unlocked the back doors.

Peter began to truly worry now. He had never been in a police car before and had no idea where they were going. As Peter and Joe approached the car, it lowered closer to the ground. Peter reached for the door handle; his hand was a little shaky. That's when he discovered there was no door handle. The door slowly opened from the bottom up. Inside, it looked like a normal back seat of any old car, but he did not see any seat belts.

"Are you getting in anytime soon?" Joe nudged him.

Peter climbed in and slid over so Joe could get in behind. When the door was completely shut, he heard a commanding female computer voice say, "Seatbelt fastening," followed by a clicking noise close to his right ear. He soon felt the strap of a seatbelt come across his chest and lap. Peter thought it was really awesome.

The police officer's voice made him look up. "I am Officer O'Bryan. Tell me your name, lad."

"It's Peter Fischer." Peter fidgeted in his seat. The officer wrote Peter's name down on a sheet of paper.

"Off we go then to the mayor's." Officer O'Bryan gestured forward.

The mayor, Peter thought to himself. *The big guy, the one who runs the town. Why do I need to go see him? What if he throws humans in jail? What if I can't ever go home?* His mind was filled with "what ifs." He changed his attention to outside the car. The squad car drove past another car, but Peter did not have a clear view inside. Then he saw a Candonite getting into his car. He was most definitely of the candy corn race. It brightened Peter's mood. The police car slowed down, and to the right was a long, rectangular, fuchsia house with a white sign out front that read "Mayor Baker." Officer O'Bryan pulled into the driveway, and the car lowered to park. The computer voice activated again: "Seatbelt unfastening," and the belt slid off Peter's chest and lap and vanished somewhere in the seat. All the doors of the car lifted up to let them out.

"All right, boys, time to see the mayor," Officer O'Bryan said as he got out of the car and waited for the boys to get out. By now, Peter's hands were sweaty and his pits were sticky. Peter could now see that Officer O'Bryan was quite tall. He knew in a fraction of a second what he was: a red licorice vine. They all walked up to the house together, and Officer O'Bryan stuck out his skinny red arm and rang the doorbell. Peter was surprised the door seemed pretty average. The same computerized woman's voice echoed throughout the house, "Attention: three guests at the door, three guests at the door." Peter wanted to push the doorbell again. He didn't dare.

Seconds later, they heard a gentle female voice from within the house saying, "Coming, dears."

Peter's tense shoulders took a more natural position. In the doorway, a pleasant-looking Candonite faced them. She smelled wonderful, like fresh-baked cake. Her smile was gigantic, and her hair was vanilla frosting. She was obviously a cupcake woman, a beautiful, friendly, sweet cupcake woman.

"Hello, Officer O'Bryan, Joe, and who do we have here?" she asked sweetly, looking directly at Peter.

"Peter," he answered.

"Nice to meet you, Peter. I am Mrs. Baker." Her eyes seemed to twinkle. "Come on in," she said, turning around to allow her guests to follow her into the living room.

There were pictures hanging in the hallway of all different Candonites. One was a photo of Officer O'Bryan and Mrs. Baker. In the middle was a cupcake man with chocolate frosting hair. Peter thought that must be Mr. Baker, the mayor. A photo next to it was a picture of Mrs. Baker in her younger days, looking rather lovely with an elegant sash strung across her chest reading "Ms. Congeniality." He was not sure what "congeniality" meant, but it must have been something good because she looked proud.

On a red velvet couch in the living room, reading a newspaper, sat the same cupcake man Peter had seen in the hallway photo.

The man closed his newspaper and rose from the couch, saying cheerfully, "Hello there, fellows." He paused to hear their greetings before he continued, "Who do we have here?" studying Peter.

Joe promptly piped up, "I found him, Mayor Baker. His name is Peter."

Peter looked over at Joe, who was beaming with pride.

"I see. There will be a parade as usual. It has been a while since we have had a parade in Maple Town, hasn't it?"

Maple Town. That sounds pleasant, Peter thought.

"I will let the Parade Council know immediately," Officer O'Bryan announced and quickly went on his way, taking Mrs. Baker's hand in his and kissing the top of it as he left the room. Peter had seen his uncle do this to his mother and grandmother millions of times before.

"A parade for me?" inquired Peter.

"Of course. We do that for all our human friends," said Mayor Baker.

Joe boasted, "You aren't the first human here, and you won't be the last. Mostly we get children, and a few adults. They all have come the same way, you know, by Bellyache."

"By Bellyache?"

Joe explained, "Yes. You probably got here by gorging yourself with tons of goodies and making yourself sick to your stomach, and next thing you knew, you were here, and..."

"That's enough, Joe," Mayor Baker interrupted firmly. Joe crossed his arms and pouted. "How old are you, Peter?"

"Ten."

"Why, you're only a year younger than Joe," Mayor Baker pointed out. "Let me tell you something. You don't have to worry about a thing. You will be in town for about twenty-four hours and then you should be on your way home. You will stay here with Mrs. Baker and me. We have a nice room that would be perfect for you."

Peter did not know what to say. So much was going through his head. The only thing he could think to say was, "Thank you."

Mayor Baker looked at the clock on the wall and said, "Let me show you to your room so you can rest a little bit and get washed up for dinner." He turned to Joe and said admiringly, "Nice work, Joe. We will see you tomorrow."

Joe shot a quick look at Peter before he left, the kind of look older kids usually give younger kids that says, "I am going to give you trouble just because you are younger and I can."

Mrs. Baker announced cheerfully that she would start dinner and disappeared down the end of the hall. Mayor Baker led Peter up the stairs to his room. It was a spacious room with a big bed and a comfy-looking chair. A wooden dresser and a wicker wastebasket were across from the bed and chair. There was also a side table next to the bed that had a funky-looking lamp on it. A few decorations hung on the wall: marshmallow bird paintings and pretty stained-glass pieces. He also had a bathroom, one all to himself. It wasn't exactly his style, but it was suitable for Peter.

"We will call on you when it is time for dinner. I understand you may not be very hungry after all you have eaten to get here." Peter was a little embarrassed by this remark. "So, don't worry about hurting the Mrs.' feelings if you don't eat much." On his way out, he showed Peter how the lights worked. There was a small circle on the wall next to the door, and he simply touched it to switch the funky lamp on and off. Mayor Baker closed the door behind him.

As soon as the door shut, Peter tried out the light circle. On and off, on and off, and on and off again. He wondered what Candonites ate and if he would like dinner. He sat on the comfy chair and studied the room and replayed the day's events in his head. Would anyone believe him when he told about this adventure? By now, Papa must have gone back to the sweet shop to look for him, but he obviously wouldn't find Peter there. Would Peter believe someone else if they told him they had met Candonites and petted a peppermint cat? He really wasn't sure. He sat there for several minutes, his head full of thoughts about his situation. He got up and noticed a book on the bedside table. The book looked weathered and read "Guests" in cursive across the cover. He opened it. Page after page was filled with names, some much more legible than others. There must have been hundreds. He turned to the page that had the last signed name on it. He wanted to put his name in the book, too, as proof he was there. He saw a pen next to the lamp and signed his name in cursive: Peter Fischer.

"Dinner is ready; please attend," came the computerized woman's voice.

Peter put the book and pen down, quickly washed his hands, and went to the dining room. It took him a little while to find it since Mayor Baker had forgotten to tell him where it was. The sweet scent of the Bakers was masked by the smell of a home-cooked meal. He was pretty sure he smelled mashed potatoes. As Peter entered the dining room, he saw a round table with eight chairs. The mayor was already seated.

"Have a seat, Peter, anywhere you like."

He sat two seats down from the mayor in case Mrs. Baker wanted to sit between them. He also did not want to be too far in case someone wanted to pass him something. As soon as Peter was seated, the phone rang. It made him jump a little.

Mayor Baker rose, calling to the kitchen, "I'll get it."

Peter watched him go to the corner of the room where there was a brass stand with a black cordless phone on it. Peter wasn't impressed. He expected something more like a circle on the table that you could just touch to receive a phone call.

He heard Mayor Baker's end of the conversation. "Hello. How are you, Angela? You heard correctly. Judge Greg's house will do just fine. Be sure to inform the council. Good work, and good night."

Peter was admiring the table when the mayor returned to his chair. He saw that he was indeed correct; there were mashed potatoes in a lopsided, multicolored ceramic bowl on the table. A gravy boat sat next to it, and salt and pepper shakers shaped similarly to the bowl. The table wasn't set, and there was nothing to drink on the table. Mrs. Baker emerged from the kitchen with a push cart with two shelves. The lower shelf had glasses containing water, plates, and silverware, which were all lopsided like their mates on the table. The upper shelf carried yet another matching covered dish and crisp white cloth napkins. Peter was a little nervous. What could be under there? He watched as she had the table set in no time.

Mrs. Baker turned to Peter and said, "I will let you serve yourself since I don't know how much you would like." Peter hadn't really thought about it; he wasn't full anymore but he wasn't starving, either. He would have a small serving of the potatoes. He wasn't sure about whatever was under that lid. Mrs. Baker handed him the serving spoon to scoop up his potatoes. She then put her dainty fingers around the handle of the lid to reveal the hidden dish. Peter held his breath. A ham, a lovely ham.

"It looks great, dear." Mayor Baker winked at his wife.

"Yes, it sure does." Peter was relieved.

Peter scooped himself a nice portion of potatoes and took a small piece of ham. He poured gravy over both. Then he realized there were no vegetables on his plate—nothing green, anyway. He wasn't a big fan of most vegetables, though he really enjoyed corn. At Nana's, he would always have to clean his plate. At home, he was usually good at hiding the vegetables under his last bit of food when he was done. Here, there weren't vegetables to eat or hide. He was beginning to really like staying with the Bakers.

"I have also made your favorite dessert," Mrs. Baker told her husband. Her husband grabbed her hand and gave it a squeeze. Peter thought he better save a tiny bit of room so he could at least taste the mayor's favorite dessert.

"Peter, I figured after dinner we would drive around for a little tour of our town. Then we could come back and watch one of my favorite game shows. The Mrs. and I love game shows. All those violent TV programs are not for us. After that, you can turn in to your room for the night. Tomorrow is an exciting day for you," Mayor Baker informed him.

Peter replied eagerly, "Sounds great."

Over dinner, which was quite good, Mayor Baker and the Mrs. asked Peter questions about where he was from and what his family was like. He also learned that the Bakers did not have any children and were trying to adopt a baby. Mrs. Baker showed him a picture of the little tyke. Peter saw that it was a tiny chocolate chip cookie baby lying on a pink blanket. It was a baby girl they wanted to name Robin after Mayor Baker's beloved grandmother. Peter told them the baby was cute and he thought it was great that they were adopting. He mused for an instant and realized it did not even seem weird that he was commenting on a cookie baby!

"Time for dessert," Mrs. Baker announced as she got up and started putting the dishes back on the push cart. Peter and Mayor Baker helped out by passing her the things on the table. When she returned with the dessert, Peter saw that it was a pie. He would have a thin slice. He did not want to be rude, after all.

"You may not like this, dear," Mrs. Baker warned as she cut into the pie. As she sliced it open, Peter smelled something downright stinky.

"What is it?" Peter asked politely.

"It is double layer Brussels sprout pie," Mrs. Baker answered.

Peter's eyes widened with shock. He did not think about it before. Why would it be anything other than a vegetable pie? After all, Candonites were probably not cannibals. How silly of him.

"You may pass on dessert if you'd like," she said kindly.

"Thank you; I will pass," he said, relieved. Brussels sprouts to him were the most disgusting vegetables ever. There was no way he wanted that pie anywhere near his mouth.

Mayor Baker said sincerely, "It must be very strange for you, meeting us Candonites." Peter nodded, and Mayor Baker reflected, "I remember when I met my first human, Christopher. He was about your age, and I was only five years old. I was in my own surroundings, and it was hard for me to comprehend a human in my town. It has to be harder for you, being away from your home and in a strange place. It was difficult for me to understand, not to mention how extremely frightened I was when Christopher explained to me that where you are from, you eat things that look like us. I understand now that they aren't alive, they fit on a plate, and do not have feelings or Candonite emotions. There were a few bites too over the years, fortunately not to me or the Mrs. The bites were given by younger human children and one crazy adult, but no real harm has ever been done. I guess their curiosity got the best of them."

"That's why Joe told me not to bite him," Peter recalled.

Mayor and Mrs. Baker laughed. Peter laughed, too. Peter tried respectfully not to get grossed out as the Bakers enjoyed their dessert. Afterwards, they cleaned up together. Peter's mother always told him that if he is invited to a nice dinner someone has thoughtfully prepared, the least he can do is help with the clean up.

The Tour

"Let's be on our way to give you your tour of our Maple Town," Mayor Baker said.

Peter followed the Bakers to their garage and got in their car, which was smaller than Officer O'Bryan's and ruby red. In tighter quarters, the Bakers' pleasant odor filled the air. He thought of his father and how much he would like this car. His father's favorite car color was red. He wished his father was with him now. He thought he would get along with the Bakers nicely.

Out of curiosity, Peter couldn't keep from looking into every car they passed. The Bakers showed him the major shopping center, which contained a movie theater. The buildings of the center were vibrant colors and were all stacked together. The parking lot was half full. They drove by the movie theater and saw a couple of signs for movies playing. One was a love story with a picture of a male and a female Candonite staring into each other's eyes. The female was a glamorous strawberry woman with what looked like chocolate hair. The male was obviously a handsome speckled jelly bean. The second sign was for a dinosaur movie. The stars appeared to be giant gummies, an enormous

Tyrannosaurus Rex, and a fierce Velociraptor. Peter decided he wouldn't mind seeing the dinosaur movie but definitely wouldn't want to see the love story—no way!

The next stop was a place called Glovers Park. It was where the Bakers went on picnics with friends. It was mostly empty, but there were a few town residents walking their dogs. The trees and grass made it an especially blue-green park. The sun was setting. Peter could see in the distance a round blue frame of a Candonite standing in the warmth of the lowering rays. Soon it would be dark.

"Before it gets dark, we should show you Old Town. That is where our library and Maple Town Museum are located," Mayor Baker suggested.

"Okay!" Peter replied. He was thoroughly enjoying himself.

Old Town was quaint, and the business buildings were much shorter than the ones at the mall. They weren't all connected to each other like the mall, but they were close, with only a few feet between them. The buildings here were much duller compared to those in the rest of the town. Paint was peeling off some of the buildings.

They drove by the library and the museum, both of which were closed. In the middle of Old Town, they came to a crosswalk where the mayor had to stop to let an elderly faded green gumdrop man cross the street. Peter was fascinated by the fact that the old gumdrop man had only one leg and hobbled along with a crutch. He was cheery despite having one leg. The old gumdrop man flashed a genuine smile and wave of thanks to the mayor when he passed by.

On the way back to the Bakers' house, they stopped in front of Maple Town School. It was a friendly looking place with a stone sculpture of the letters "MTS" positioned in the middle of the courtyard. It was an extreme yellow and orange hexagon building that looked like a fun place to go to school. Peter imagined attending the school with all the Candonite children. How awesome would that be?

"All school-age children attend classes here," the mayor informed him.

Last stop was Town Hall. It was a large, glass, stop-sign-shaped building with many steps leading to the front entrance. A cleaning van that read "Lemony Fresh Cleaners" was parked out front.

"That car belongs to Joe's father. Real nice fella who does darn good work." That was a far cry from what Peter thought Joe's dad would be like—a mean old bear.

"Is this where you work?" inquired Peter.

"Yup, my office is right in the middle on the fourth floor." Mayor Baker pointed upward.

On the way home, almost dark now, they passed by the Bakers' favorite restaurant, Bella's House of Food. It was a huge, silvery-white dome and the windows were all different shapes, sizes, and colors: tiny purple star windows, large orange oval windows, red diamond windows—so many different ones. It looked like a pretty interesting place. According to the Bakers, it had the best food around.

Mrs. Baker said in a voice like a commercial announcer, "They serve a side of fun with every meal!"

"I have an idea. Why don't we meet for lunch tomorrow and go to Bella's? I should be able to take off work for a bit," the mayor suggested.

"That would be a real treat for Peter." The Mrs. turned to look at Peter in the backseat. "How about it?"

Peter said excitedly, "I can't wait!"

Nosey Neighbor and a Good Poke

Upon returning from the tour and pulling into the driveway of the Bakers' house, Peter spotted two figures standing next to the mailbox.

As they approached, Mrs. Baker let out a quiet, "Oh dear."

Mayor Baker warned as they approached the figures, "Now, Peter, don't mind Carol Winston; she's a true busybody, and that is her nephew, Poke. He's a good boy."

Poke. Had he heard Mayor Baker right? If so, that was a very interesting name. Peter could make out the figures now. He saw that Carol Winston was unmistakably a candy cane lady: red and white. And Poke was what appeared to be a chocolate candy cup of some sort. Could he possibly be...probably not. Poke was smiling joyfully, but Carol Winston was not, her stern face lit from the outside lights. Her look forced him to look straight at the back of Mayor Baker's head.

The car pulled into the driveway and everyone got out. Carol Winston and Poke waited patiently at the garage.

"We went to the door and discovered you weren't home," Carol informed them.

Tolerating her, Mayor Baker said, "Yes, Carol, we were out showing Peter the town."

"Oh, Peter is his name, eh." She eyed Peter up and down.

Peter was very uncomfortable.

Mrs. Baker piped in, "Hello, Poke. Nice to see you. How long are you visiting?

"Nice to see you, too. My mom is picking me up the day after tomorrow," he replied.

"I have an idea. How about coming with us to Bella's House of Food for lunch tomorrow? I know how much you love it there—if that is okay with your aunt, of course." Mrs. Baker looked at Carol.

"You know where I stand on that issue, Sandy...but as I always say, I am not the boss of anyone, and he has his own mind to make up. But if he loses a finger, he better not come crying to me!" Carol Winston grumbled.

"Nonsense, Carol, no one will be losing any fingers," Mayor Baker insisted. Carol's red and white eyebrows lowered.

"Tomorrow for lunch, all right!" Poke said cheerfully.

"Wonderful," Mrs. Baker replied.

Carol Winston crossed her arms and mumbled something under her breath.

"We better be getting inside. We don't want to miss our favorite show." Mr. Baker began walking backward toward the front door. Mrs. Baker followed, and Peter wasn't about to stay there, so he followed them as well. They all waved and said good night except for Carol Winston, who was still pouting and scowling at Peter. She made Peter's skin crawl.

Once inside, Mayor Baker whispered, "As I said before, Peter, don't pay her any mind. She is a little unreasonable and a wee bit eccentric." He winked at Peter. Peter gave a half smile back, still uncomfortable from the encounter.

"Only five minutes until *Journey to Your Future*," Mrs. Baker chimed in.

Sitting on the velvet couch between the Bakers, Peter took a sweet, deep breath and almost had to pinch himself to assure he was really there. Would anyone believe him? He almost did not care either way. He knew the truth.

Journey to Your Future was a fun game show to watch. There was a contestant named Pearl and a host named Jabber James. "Jabber" suited him well. He was a real talker. His hair stood straight up on his head, and was striped pale pink, light blue, and crisp white. Peter thought he resembled cotton candy. Pearl looked like candy corn. She was super excited, clapping her hands and waving them all around.

The stage held what Jabber James announced as the "Journey Center." It was five stories high with eight small rooms side by side on each level. Each room had four doors: two on opposite walls and one on the ceiling and one on the floor. Every room was decorated with a different theme, from a pirate's cove to a princess's chambers.

The object of the game was for the contestants to pick the right path to eventually arrive in the room that held the key to their future. During Pearl's journey, she would come across keys and have to decide whether or not to keep that particular key or to continue searching through the Journey Center until she found another one. There were only three keys in the Journey Center, all located in different rooms. Only one key held the wealthiest future. The other two could be splendid prizes or disappointing junk. Along the way, she might find prizes, which she had to open up and show the audience before moving on through her journey if she wanted to keep them. And she only had ten minutes in which to do it.

Pearl raced through those rooms with tremendous speed, climbing up and down ladders to reach the doors and get to different rooms. Peter thought she had impressive agility for someone her shape, triangular and all. She stopped and made sure to open every prize she found. The biggest prize she found was in the jungle room: a bag of gold coins worth two thousand dollars. Peter thought he could do a whole mess with that sort of money and soon found himself imagining it was him up there in the Journey Center on a quest for his future. Pearl stuck with the first key she discovered in the Egyptian room and informed everyone in an out-of-breath scream that it was the key to her future!

Jabber started with the two keys Pearl did not choose. The first key unlocked a chest that contained free movie tickets for five years. Imagine going to see all the movies you wanted for free! Peter thought you could definitely afford popcorn then! The second key unlocked jet skis. Wow, jet skis would be great fun; he and Lina could go to the lake and ride them all day long. Peter thought those were pretty big prizes. He wondered what was left for Pearl. The mayor and the Mrs. were practically on the edge of their seats. Peter was caught up in all the excitement when Jabber James jerked his head toward the camera and announced another commercial break.

"Oh, crumbles!" Mayor Baker protested. "Every week they take a commercial break at that exact time, and every week it tricks me!" Peter and Mrs. Baker laughed. The phone rang, and Mrs. Baker got up gracefully to answer it. She quickly handed it off to the mayor, and Peter heard this part of the conversation:

"Judge Greg, how are you this evening? We are watching the same thing, so we'll be quick. Yes, tomorrow we are going to Bella's for lunch. Great, then I won't see you there. I will see you at the parade. Have a wonderful night! Good-bye." Mayor Baker hung up swiftly.

"Great, I won't see you there." *What an odd thing to say*, thought Peter.

Jabber James's voice drew Peter's attention back to the TV. What was Pearl taking home?

"Oh, I hope they don't do what they did last week." Mrs. Baker sounded a little concerned. She turned to Peter and said, "The contestant won a bar of soap a year for ten years. Isn't that just awful?"

Peter thought Pearl seemed like a nice Candonite and she deserved more than a dumb bar of soap. They all watched intently as Pearl turned the key that held her future. Peter imagined it was him holding that key, and he wanted to win something totally outrageous.

As Jabber James read aloud what she had won, Peter felt like he was there. Jabber James was giving him the prize.

"Peter, your future holds for you..." Peter winced as Jabber went on in an enormous voice, "one new car every year, for the next five years!" Peter and everyone cheered "Wait! There is more!" *No way! Awesome*, thought Peter, "Twenty thousand dollars a year for the next five years!"

"Those are definitely grand prizes," stated the mayor.

"How lovely for her!" Mrs. Baker added.

"I could do a lot with that kind of cash!" Peter confessed.

"I bet you could. What would be the first thing you would buy?" inquired a giggling Mrs. Baker.

"Well," Peter thought hard for a moment, "I know." He touched his chin. "I would buy a sports store. And it would have to have batting cages so my friends and I could hit some balls whenever we felt like it. Yeah, a sports store! My dad and I could run it, and I would always have the sporting gear I needed. I always need a different size these days. My mom says I am growing like a weed, and I always have to wait until the first of the month for clothes, like sweat pants or a new jersey that fits. If I owned a sports store, I would take it off the rack and wear it out of the store because I could."

"Jolly idea! I like it: a young business man." Mayor Baker applauded.

"I believe you and your father would enjoy that very much," said a smiling Mrs. Baker.

"This is where we turn in for the night, son," Mayor Baker stated, rising off the couch. "I know it seems early. But the Mrs. likes to read her books, and I always go over my work for the next day before we go to bed."

"You may stay up and watch more television, or there are some books in the side table by your bed; you are more than welcome to read one if you would like. Oh, and there is a toothbrush and toothpaste for you in the medicine cabinet in the bathroom," Mrs. Baker said as she rose from the couch.

After saying their good nights, Mrs. Baker reminded him as his own mother would, "Don't stay up too late."

The Bakers started to leave the room when Peter said, "I had a great time tonight; thank you for everything." And he really meant it. He needed to say it just in case he went to bed and woke up the next morning somewhere other than Maple Town.

"Our pleasure, my boy, our pleasure," said the mayor.

Mrs. Baker beamed at Peter and then turned to her husband, and Peter saw for a moment a brief frown tinged with sadness. The mayor gently took her hand and led her out of the room.

She will miss me when I am gone, Peter thought. He remembered what the mayor had said when Peter had met him: "You will be in town for about twenty-four hours and then you'll be on your way home." He sat there mindlessly flipping through the channels, watching different shows, everything from infomercials to a detective movie. The next thing he knew, two hours had passed. Peter turned off the TV and quietly moved through the house to his room. He listened carefully and heard no noises except for the ones he was making himself. The Bakers had gone to sleep. Peter reached his room and swiped on the light. He closed the door softly and realized he was not one bit tired. He was excited for tomorrow's events and at the same time worried. What if he went to bed and woke up in the morning and was not in Maple Town anymore and did not get to say good-bye?

The Guest Book

In the bathroom, Peter opened the medicine cabinet and found a toothbrush and toothpaste. He examined the toothbrush; the head was twice the size of the one he had at home. He hadn't thought of it before but now it occurred to him that the Candonites' mouths were bigger than human mouths. He took the toothpaste out and examined it as well.

He read the label of the toothpaste under his breath: "Spinach Delight, the perfect flavor to wake up your mouth!"

"Disgusting!" exclaimed Peter, and his face turned a shade of green. He covered his mouth when he realized he may have said that loud enough to disturb the Bakers.

Out of curiosity, Peter unscrewed the cap and squirted a glob across the bristles of the toothbrush. The glob was light green with specks of dark green, and it smelled dreadful, like cooked spinach. "Uh uh. No way. I am not putting that in my mouth," he muttered as he shook his head fiercely.

He quickly rinsed off the end of the toothbrush and shoved it back in the medicine cabinet with the toothpaste. He brushed his teeth with his index finger and water. "There, good enough," he whispered triumphantly.

He crossed the room to the side table and opened the drawer to find several books. He took them out one at a time and piled them on the bed: an adventure novel, a girl book, a mystery novel, and a handful more. He sorted through the books until he figured he wasn't in a reading mood. Besides, he wouldn't get to finish a book, anyway. He put them all back. His eyes caught a glimpse of the guest book. He picked it up and plopped down on the bed with his legs crossed. He turned the pages slowly, looking at the different names. He saw a name he rather liked.

"Willie Watson." It rolled off his tongue. He thought if his name was not Peter Fischer, it would suit him well.

Peter wondered if Willie was a boy like him— maybe even perhaps in the same grade. He read some of the other names, fascinated so many were all once there before him. Eventually, Peter tired of looking through the book. He began to close it but stopped abruptly when he recognized a name. He was in disbelief as he read the name aloud. "Sasha Plunket." Nana? Could it possibly be? Sasha was Nana's first name, and Plunket was her last name before she married Papa. Peter knew this because he had seen an old newspaper clipping with a picture of a high-school-aged Nana on the swim team. They had a conversation about how she had won six swimming competitions in a row one year. Could she have been in Maple Town?

Peter whispered, "Nana, were you here?"

He wanted to rush to the Bakers' bedroom door that very instant to wake them up and ask if they knew who she was, if they remembered having met Sasha Plunket. He had both his feet off the bed when he decided it could wait until morning. He did not want to be rude and disturb them. Nana had been there—he knew it. He felt it in his gut. He would have to talk to Nana as soon as he got back home. He climbed back on the bed and lay down this time. He continued to look through the guest book to see if he recognized any other names; it took him quite some time since he read every name in the book, one by one. There must have been hundreds of them.

Peter awoke joyously in the morning to find himself still in Maple Town. He had fallen asleep with the light on and saw that the guest book was now down by his feet. He sat up, grabbed and examined the book to make sure he had not damaged it. It looked okay. He turned quickly to see if Nana's name was still there. It was. He stretched out of bed and placed the book safely back on the side table.

Peter washed up in the sink. He brushed his teeth with his finger. He had no clothes to change into, so he had to wear the clothes he had on. That did not bother him, though; he preferred it that way. If you fell asleep with your clothes on and woke up to start the day in them, it saved a lot of time. He knew his mother would never let him get away with it, though.

Downstairs, he found Mrs. Baker in the kitchen, cleaning up some of those odd-shaped dishes.

"Good morning, Peter!" Mrs. Baker sang.

"Good morning!" Peter replied, sliding onto a wide stool in front of the counter. It was definitely a good morning. He was still in Maple Town and eager for the day to go on—and eager to ask, "Do you remember a Sasha Plunket? She is my grandmother, and I saw her name written in the guest book. She was here, I just know it!"

"Sasha Plunket?" She paused to think. "I'm sorry, Peter. I don't recall anyone by that name. That book is quite old, and she may have been here long ago. If you have a gut feeling that she was here, you are probably right. How neat would that be?" She leaned forward over the counter and tapped the tip of his nose with her finger.

"That would be pretty neat!" he confessed.

"Now, how about some leftover ham slices and eggs for breakfast?" she asked.

His stomach growled, "Yes, please."

They enjoyed breakfast together and talked about all sorts of things. He learned that Mrs. Baker volunteered some of her time at the local school and read to the children every other day. Today was one of her days off. He told her that he would like it if she read for his class. Unfortunately, he also found out Candonites rarely left Maple Town or the only other neighboring town, Honeyville.

"Our world is incredibly small compared to yours, Peter. Humans have been dropping in from time to time, but a Candonite has hardly left either town. It is just as well; I don't think a Candonite would fare well in your world."

He had a picture in his mind of his favorite restaurant, which carried so many delicious desserts, and what Mrs. Baker might do if she went there and saw people stuffing their faces with them. He shook off the thought. "You might not like some things there."

They finished breakfast, and Peter helped with clean-up.

"I have a few things to do this morning. You are welcome to watch some television or go enjoy the nice weather if you would like," Mrs. Baker said.

"Okay," Peter answered.

"It will be a few hours before Gus picks us up for lunch," Mrs. Baker told him.

"Who's Gus?" Peter asked.

"Oh, pardon me. That is Mr. Baker's first name. Mine is Sandy," she smiled.

"Gus and Sandy Baker." Peter thought that sounded pleasant.

The Tin

Peter had watched about an hour of television when he heard the computerized voice say, "Attention: one guest at the door, one guest at the door."

Peter heard Mrs. Baker call out, "Coming, dear!"

Peter couldn't see the front door, so he listened intently over the television sounds. He was a bit nervous it might be Carol Winston coming over to fuss and scowl at him some more. He wouldn't mind if he never saw her again.

"How lovely to see your smiling face this morning! Come on in. Peter is in the living room," Mrs. Baker's pleasant voice rang.

He knew as soon as he heard "smiling face" that it could not possibly be Carol Winston. She had no smile lines on her face; Peter did not think she ever smiled. She only had frown lines.

Poke emerged into the living room, and Peter was happy to see him.

"Hey, I came over to see if you wanted to hang outside for a while until we go to Bella's House of Food."

"Sure, but won't your aunt mind?" Peter asked

worriedly.

"Don't worry about her, Peter; she looks much meaner than she really is. She is not fond of humans because my great-grandfather told her a story about when he was a boy and was bitten by a human who practically tore his finger off," Poke told Peter as if he had heard it a thousand times. "My mom and dad say great-grandfather was notorious for stretching the truth. But my Aunt Carol seems to believe him. She tells me not to talk to humans, but she isn't the boss of me. So if I did talk to them and lost a finger, don't come crying to her."

Peter replied, "I will keep my teeth to myself, I promise."

Outside, it was the perfect temperature, not too hot and not too cold. The sun was shining as it had been the day before, and there wasn't a cloud in the sky. Peter was thoroughly enjoying himself when an image caught the corner of his eye. A piercing glare came from the unmistakable Carol Winston from between her curtains. They locked eyes, and he felt his hair stand up on his arms. She shook her head in disapproval and shut the curtains, quick and stern. Peter shook off a shiver and turned away from the window to face Poke.

"Is Poke your real name or a nickname?"

"It's my real name. Poke is short for slow poke. My parents named me that because I was born late. My mom said I must have gotten comfortable in her tummy because I didn't want to come out; I was in there for weeks after I was supposed to be born."

Peter was amused by his story. "It's a really interesting name, that's for sure!"

"I rather like it now, but when I was younger, some older kids used to call me Hokey Pokey; I hated that. I would walk down the sidewalk, minding my own business, when I would hear them chanting, 'Okie dokie artichokie. Here he comes, it's Hokey Pokey!' I remember wishing I was bigger so I could whoop 'em good and they would never sing that dreadful song again. I guess they grew tired of making fun of me, because one day I walked by the same group and waited for that horrible chant to start. I could almost hear it before it started. But it never did start and hasn't since." Poke shrugged and added, "Maybe it was because I grew five and a half inches that year and I was as tall as the tallest of 'em."

"I know what you mean. When I was younger, I had the same problem with this girl named Henrietta. She used to drive me nuts! Whenever I ran into her, she would holler, 'Peter Fischer, come here and give me a great big kisser!'"

Poke burst out laughing! Peter was initially offended by his outburst because, after all, he did not laugh at Poke's story.

By now, Poke's round body was doubled over with laughter, and he was apologizing for his rudeness in between giant gasps for air. "I'm sorry...it's just that...that Henrietta...was saying that because...she had a crush on you...and she had a very inventive way of letting you know it!"

Peter joined in with Poke's laughter. It may not have been funny at the time when Henrietta's red curls bounced up and down as she pointed her finger at him, but it did seem funny now.

"I've got something I'd like to show ya. Follow me," Poke said, tugging on Peter's shirt sleeve.

They walked behind creepy Carol Winston's house. They ventured a few yards, turned left, and disappeared behind a huge blue-green bush. Peter could no longer see the houses and suspected no one in the houses could see them, either. The bush stood about four inches taller than Peter and about six feet wide. Poke sat down and stuck his arm into the massive bush, feeling around for something. His arm reappeared with a small white tin with "Candonites" printed all over it.

"Sit down." He gestured toward the long blades of blue-green grass.

The grass was comfortable and cool on Peter's legs. Intrigued, Peter watched as Poke carefully opened his tin.

Poke's cheerful face became extremely serious. Almost whispering, he advised, "Now, these are my most prized possessions. I will show you, but ya have to promise to be careful with them."

Peter gulped and whispered back, "I will."

Poke turned the box toward Peter. Peter gazed inside the tin, and his eyes locked in on every object:

a splendid golden coin with a distinguished-looking Candonite carved into it, a plastic baggie with little green shriveled balls inside, a newspaper clipping, a torn white piece of paper, and a slender wooden cylinder.

"I take these with me when I'm going to be away from home. Bless my aunt, but she is one of the nosiest people ever born. I hide it out here so she doesn't go snooping around in it."

Peter remarked, "This is a great hiding place."

Poke took the shriveled green things out of the tin and opened the plastic bag. "These are dried green peas, my favorite."

"Dried green peas are your favorite? Are you kidding?" As Peter said this, he remembered Sandy Baker's dessert the night before, Brussels sprout pie, and realized he wasn't kidding.

"Nope, they are my favorite," Poke confirmed.

"Sorry about that," Peter explained. "Where I come from, I doubt anyone would say peas are their favorite food."

"No problem. I know."

Moving on, Poke turned their attention back to the tin. "This," he said, taking out the golden coin, "is a gift from my dad." He handed the coin to Peter so he could get a closer look.

"Wow, is this what Candonites use to buy things with? Is this money?"

"Naw, that is not money, although it is very precious to me. That Candonite you see carved in the coin is my dad. He had it made at the town fair two years ago."

"I like it. It's a cool gift; your dad looks very smart. Is he?" Peter asked.

"He sure was. The smartest!" Poke remarked with pride.

"Was?"

"Yeah, my old man died last year," Poke spoke softly, taking the coin back to admire it.

"I'm sorry," Peter said sympathetically. Until then, Peter never even associated a Candonite with being able to die. They seemed so magical, so eternal.

"Ah, don't feel sorry for me; I don't. He was the best dad in all of Honeyville and Maple Town put together! We had some really great times. My dad was such a fun guy to be around. He loved playing practical jokes on people. He would let me get in on some of the jokes sometimes. One time, we even played a practical joke on Aunt Carol."

"Really? That's brave!" Peter exclaimed. "I bet she didn't like that at all."

"How'd you guess? I can tell you one thing, we never played one on her again."

"Tell me about it," Peter begged.

Poke sat up straight and leaned in toward Peter. "Well, one afternoon three summers ago while we were here visiting Aunt Carol, Dad conjured up this grand idea. He had this glint in his eyes, the same glint he'd get every time he had a super joke to tell or a crazy prank to play on an unsuspecting victim. This time, his victim was my cranky aunt. I told him I didn't think it was a good idea, but he would hear nothing of it.

"We waited until mom went for her afternoon jog and Aunt Carol stepped outside to fetch the mail. Dad had me watch at the front window to make sure we had enough time to set up." By now, Peter was so enthralled by Poke's marvelous story he did not even notice a milk chocolate bunny go hopping by. "Dad ran to the kitchen, got out a white paper bag, and with the speed of lightning, cut out two circles for eyes with a pair of scissors. He grabbed two markers, one blood red and one black, and swiftly created his masterpiece..."

"What was he creating?" Peter interrupted.

"An evil clown."

"A clown!"

"Aunt Carol despises clowns. She thinks they are annoying creatures who are useless to society. She wouldn't even come to my fifth birthday party when my parents hired a clown for entertainment. We didn't miss her much anyway, to tell you the truth. She would have just complained about Mr. Happiness being there—that was the clown's name. Anyway, back to my story. Dad grabbed a flashlight from the drawer and called out to me to ask how much time we had. 'Not much,' I told him. 'She is headed this way.' Dad ran for the closet, and before putting his masterpiece inside, he showed me. I tell you, Peter, it was the scariest clown I've ever seen, even if it was made out of a paper bag.

"My dad went into the hallway closet. 'Hurry,' I whispered, 'she is almost here.' It was so close I cringed. He balanced the flashlight facing up on the shelf and placed the paper bag clown over it. The eyes beamed with glorious devilish light. Dad emerged empty-handed just as Aunt Carol opened the door. Aunt Carol and I stood face-to-face. I impulsively said to her, 'I was just coming to ask you where the broom is so I can sweep some crumbs off the floor.'

"'You were, were you? It is about time you did something helpful around here,' she croaked.

"She pointed to where my father had been just moments before. He had since made his way to the couch. 'It is in that closet.'

"My father responded slyly, 'I didn't see it in there.'

"'Oh honestly, do I have to do everything around here?' she said. She trotted over to the closet as my father and I stared.

"She swung the closet open and screamed a scream of a hundred banshees! The mail she was holding flew in all directions. One piece even landed in my dad's lap. I was too afraid to laugh so I only laughed inside.

"My dad, however, laughed so hard he cried! I thought that was enough for both of us. My aunt was so upset, she was bent over gasping for air. I thought she might pass out.

"No such luck. As my dad used to tell the story: like a wild, ravenous boar, she rose up, and with the force of a thousand roaring lions, she screamed, 'Oh, you think this is funny, do you? You won't think it's so funny when I am through with the two of you!'"

"What did she do to you?" Peter asked, wide-eyed.

"She made us sweep the whole house from top to bottom, including the garage, twice! When my aunt tells you to do something, you usually do it or you'll have to hear about it over and over and over again. She made sure to inspect our work. It really wasn't too bad, though; my mom made us a snack and something to drink. We ate it over the garbage can to make sure we didn't spill any crumbs. To tell you the truth, Peter, it was worth it just to be a part of one of my dad's famous pranks. It was really something."

Peter could tell Poke truly admired his dad. "Your dad sounds like he was a load of fun."

"And then some," Poke added.

"I have to admit, I would have liked to have seen that."

Both boys chuckled.

Taking the newspaper clipping out of the box, almost respectfully, Poke said with excitement, "Read this, Peter."

Peter took the paper from Poke and read it out loud:

REAL-LIFE SUPERHERO, RIGHT HERE IN HONEYVILLE!

By Craig Scott

Walter Hammerstein is responsible for courageously and dynamically saving a distressed little Suzanne Anderson from certain death. The six-year-old was crossing the street after looking both ways just as her parents, Hamilton and Suzette Anderson, have always taught her to do, when suddenly a limousine's hover mechanism malfunctioned and headed ferociously towards helpless little Suzanne at barreling speeds. Onlooker Walter Hammerstein risked life and limb to sweep little Suzanne out of danger's way, and he did not forget the endangered driver behind the wheel of the limousine. Walter

> **"Walter is my very best hero."**
> **Suzanne Anderson**

managed to grab hold of one of the passing limousine's door handles and window and swung himself into it. He pushed the driver, Theodore Douglas, out of the car onto a bed of grass and jumped out himself just before the limousine crashed into an enormous tree.

Witnesses say it was like watching a real-life superhero fly in to save the day. The mayor of Honeyville will be presenting Walter Hammerstein with a Good Samaritan Award. Little Suzanne Anderson was quoted as saying, "Walter is my very best hero."

"That goes for me, too," stated an extremely grateful Theodore Douglas.

"Wow that is some story," Peter commented, noticing Poke's gigantic smile.

"That is a story about my dad," Poke said, beaming with pride.

"That's awesome!" Peter said admiringly. He took a moment and imagined himself in Mr. Hammerstein's shoes, saving Suzanne and Theodore. He wondered if it was something he could have done; probably not. He wasn't as brave as Poke's dad.

"My old man made this for me," Poke said,

taking out the wooden object and the piece of paper.

"What is it?" Peter asked, admiring the sleek, smooth look of the well-crafted piece.

"It's a spitfire wooden straw. My dad made it because I would always chew on the plastic straws and destroy them. You wad up a piece of paper and stick it in your mouth, chew it for a few seconds to get it all wet, stick it in one end of the straw, blow air real hard in the other end, and out comes the paper at whatever target you have chosen."

"A spit wad!" Peter had seen spit wads from plastic straws in the school lunch room before, but never a wooden one. *What a great idea.*

"Exactly!" Poke replied.

"Can I try it out?" Peter asked eagerly.

"That's what it's for. Let's start shootin'!" Poke exclaimed.

They shot around for a while and made sure to stay behind the bush so Carol Winston couldn't see and make them stop. They did make sure to clean up as many of the spit wads as they could find afterward. They talked more about their families, friends, school, and the usual stuff, and before they knew it, it was time to go to Bella's House of Food. After all that horsing around, they decided they both had ginormous appetites and agreed they would be eating tons of food at Bella's.

Peter reminded Poke, "Let's not get belly-aches." The two new pals laughed merrily.

Bella's House of Food

The mayor picked up Mrs. Baker, Poke, and Peter. While the car hovered out of the driveway, Peter felt Carol's burning eyes on him. He knew if he turned to look at the window, she would be there, no doubt sneering and watching him drive away. He dared not look. He shivered from head to toe. He sure was delighted she wouldn't be joining them for lunch.

Bella's parking lot was full. "Everyone knows that when there is a full parking lot at a restaurant, it's got to be good." Mr. Baker said.

Peter hoped they would be able to find a spot soon. He was stricken with hunger. The mayor drove directly to an open parking space in front of the restaurant door and parked. *Lucky spot*, Peter thought. Once outside the car, he saw the burger-shaped sign that read, "Reserved for the Mayor."

When they opened the lime green diamond-shaped doors, Peter was overwhelmed by the fabulous smells: some sweet, some savory. Peter figured the sweet smells were from the Candonites themselves. The entrance was packed full of waiting Candonites. It was impossible to see past them. *Great*, thought Peter, *now I'll starve to death.*

"Not to worry," Mrs. Baker said to Peter as if she could read his mind.

Within moments the Candonites stepped off to the sides to make a clear path. Peter followed the others in amazement. "It must be another one of the mayor's perks," he whispered.

He heard voices saying, "Fine day, mayor." "Hello, mayor." "You look lovely today, Mrs. Baker." A handful of Candonites said hello to Peter, as well, and he was surprised that no one stared at him like he did not belong. If a Candonite was to walk into a restaurant back home, Peter was sure there would be some staring going on, as well as some mouths hanging open, forks falling to the ground, waitresses over-pouring water glasses, and a crazy lady in the corner screaming, "Alien! Alien!" No, the Candonites were not like that. He felt especially comfortable and welcomed.

The restaurant owner, Bella herself, greeted the mayor's group. She was an older Candonite woman with the smooth curves of a donut. She had a hole in the middle of her stomach you could see right through, multicolored sprinkles and everything.

"Where would you like to be seated today?" Bella asked in a raspy voice. Peter thought she sounded a lot like the lunch lady at school.

Mrs. Baker said, "We will let our guest pick today." She turned to Peter and then gestured towards the dining area.

Peter's eyes widened as he scanned the vast

dining area. It was truly captivating; he saw what must have been close to three hundred Candonites enjoying their lunch in such an unusual place. He had never seen any restaurant quite like this.

From behind him Poke said, "You get to choose what part of the house you want to dine in. Pretty neat, huh?"

It was more than that; it was super cool! thought Peter.

He saw brilliant signs above each section that read different parts of an actual house: bathroom, living room, dining room, kitchen, bedroom, study, laundry room, and even garden. Exactly as the names of the rooms stated, the décor matched in an exaggerated style. In the bathroom, Candonites sat happily on closed toilet seats, wiping their faces with toilet paper for napkins; in the bedroom, Candonites were being served while relaxing in beds, propped up by lush pillows; in the kitchen, Candonites sat on mini-refrigerators and mini-stoves, wearing aprons instead of bibs, among thousands of refrigerator magnets. Everyone looked thrilled to be dining at Bella's. There was so much to look at, so much going on. It was an exhilarating information overload. How could he choose among all these enchanting rooms?

"Where shall we sit, Brussels sprout?" Mrs. Baker said, encouraging him to make his choice. "I don't care where you choose, just not the bathroom. I simply can't dine sitting on a toilet!"

He was so engrossed in what was going on, he

hardly noticed that he had been called Brussels sprout, which he knew Mrs. Baker meant as a term of endearment.

"The laundry room," he blurted out. It was the room he was staring at when she asked him.

"Good choice!" Poke assured him.

The tables were made of an old-fashioned washboard lying on its side, with clear plastic laid over it. The napkins were in fabric softener boxes. Salt, pepper, ketchup, and mustard were all in liquid detergent bottles. Washers and dryers lined one of the walls. Sheets, pillow cases, towels, rugs, and curtains hung from the ceiling on thin clotheslines. No clothes. Candonites did not wear clothes, so there was no need to wash any. It wasn't odd. It seemed natural for them not to have on clothes. They would look ridiculous with them on, Peter thought.

Bella seated them on huge, colorful laundry detergent boxes and left them with dome-shaped menus which said, "A side of fun with every meal!" on the cover. He did not open the menu right away; his eyes were too busy darting around the restaurant, looking at every brilliant detail.

He saw Candonites thoroughly taking pleasure in their food, and his stomach growled viciously to remind him he was hungry. He wished he could look at the menu and the restaurant at the same time. But he knew that wasn't going to happen. So he reluctantly opened his menu to find something worthy of satisfying his hunger. There were so many choices like the Attic-ding Tuna Sandwich, the Chair-Rib Platter, and Bella's House Special Steak and Mash. He had a hard time deciding.

Bella came back. She was taking Poke's order when Peter's marvelous mood was abruptly interrupted. It was like a scene pulled right out of a movie, the kind where a bad guy comes onto the screen and everything seems to be moving in slow motion. It was Joe and what must have been Joe's father; they looked so much alike. They made their way over to the garden, diagonally across from where the Bakers were sitting. Peter followed them with his eyes. Suddenly, Joe turned his head toward their table and locked eyes with Peter. Joe took another step and was blocked by Bella's body for a second, reappearing in the center of her hole with the most dreadful face Peter had ever seen. What the heck was his problem?

"Peter?" a faint voice said.

He refocused his attention on Bella, who was talking.

"Sorry," Peter said.

"What can I get you?" she repeated herself.

"I'll have Laundry Piles of Clucks and Fries please," he answered.

"Great choice; it's one of my all-time favorites," Bella said. "And to drink, may I suggest a D.T.S? I believe you'll like it."

"D.T.S.?"

"You'll love it, I promise!" Bella insisted.

"Okay," Peter said, convinced.

Bella was off with their orders and turned around, heading straight to the garden. As soon as Bella reached her destination, she tilted her body to one side and Peter could see both Joe and his father sitting in lawn chairs on blue-green grass. Bella turned to Joe and gave him a hug only someone who knows someone very well would give. Joe glanced directly at Peter and gave him a sinister wink. It gave him chills. What was that all about? After embracing Joe, she leaned over to Joe's father and planted a kiss on his forehead, one like a mother or grand-mother would give a child.

Poke must have seen what Peter was staring at. He piped in, "That is Bella's godson, Joe, and his dad."

Peter said nothing; he did not know what to say. He wasn't sure if Joe and Poke were friends. He also did not want to trouble anyone.

His thoughts were distracted by a crying baby Candonite sitting on his mother's lap in the study. The baby's face was all squished with anguish. Peter was pretty sure they were lollipop Candonites. His mother was trying to calm him down by handing him a book from a nearby shelf to look at. It worked; he soon forgot he was upset and happily pointed to the pictures in the book. The baby glanced back at his mother with every point to make sure she was looking at the pictures with him.

A yellow haze made its way into Peter's

peripheral vision. Joe was making his way to the back of the restaurant. He waved cordially to Peter's table and smiled pleasantly at them all. Peter reluctantly waved back with the group. He followed him with his eyes until he no longer could without turning his head; then he gave in and looked over his shoulder to watch Joe fling open the tangerine doors to the restaurant's kitchen. Peter supposed Joe had the run of the whole place, seeing as how he was Bella's godson and all.

"Peter, the Mrs. tells me you think your grandmother may have been here in Maple Town. Well, I must say it is quite possible. However, I do not recall her. She may have been here before my time, or maybe I was very young then and don't remember. Sorry I couldn't be of more help to you," Mr. Baker said.

"That's all right; I understand," Peter assured him.

Bella arrived with their drink orders. She placed Peter's D.T.S. in front of him. Peter's eyebrows rose as he admired it.

"D.T.S., Dynamic Television Soda," Bella said.

"Wow!" Peter exclaimed.

The drink was served in a marvelous mini-television set with two long silver straws sticking out from the top of the TV—antennas! Peter realized his mouth was hanging open and promptly closed it.

"Go ahead, turn the knob!" Bella encouraged him.

Peter saw the knob in the lower right-hand corner and turned it clockwise. The TV screen flashed on a picture, and he could hear faint music coming out of the set. Candonites moved around the screen, dancing.

"They're music videos!" Poke told him.

"How cool is that!" Peter said, impressed.

"Now go on and taste it," Bella said, leaning in to study Peter's reaction.

He put his lips around the straw and felt all eyes at the table on him. He sucked up the liquid and braced himself in case he did not like it. He was pleasantly surprised. The sweet flavor of the soda was changing with every sip: lime, orange, cream, root beer. It was refreshing, and he did not want to stop drinking it. He forced his lips away so he could give his verdict.

"I tasted different soda flavors with every sip! It is amazing!" Peter exclaimed.

"I knew you'd love it," Bella said, tickled. "I'd best go check on your meals now."

As Bella was leaving, Joe was returning to his seat. Peter tried not to look over at him. He did not want to make eye contact again. Instead, he drank more of his D.T.S.

Bella returned carrying a large tray filled with their orders. Peter and Mrs. Baker's Piles of Clucks and Fries came in little laundry baskets. It amused Peter that Mrs. Baker had picked the same thing. Mr. Baker had ordered an Oven-Fresh Burger with a side order of Garden Macaroni Salad. The Garden Macaroni Salad came in a terracotta pot. The utensils were a miniature rake and shovel. Mr. Baker's food came in a tiny warming oven. Sitting on the top rack was a tray with a luscious burger on it, and on the rack below it were golden brown oven-baked chips. Mr. Baker explained that he wouldn't get burnt taking anything out of the oven because it was kept at a low warming temperature. *What a stupendous idea!* Peter thought. Poke's order was a Tub of Spaghetti with Meatballs, which arrived in a small porcelain bath-tub. Their waters came in measuring cups.

Some spread! Peter thought. He wished again that his family could be there with him at that moment. They would have a real blast. By the end of his adventure, Peter knew his eyes would be so dry from not blinking them as often as he should because they were so busy taking everything in.

Peter looked over at Mrs. Baker, who was thoroughly at bliss eating her food. He politely asked Poke to pass the ketchup and squeezed a dollop in the corner of his laundry basket. He was famished by now and couldn't wait to dig in. He grabbed a Cluck, dipped it in his ketchup, and began to devour it.

Hot...burning hot...fire! His eyes watered as he swallowed and he began to cough as he reached for his D.T.S. His taste buds felt like they were melting off. His nose was inflamed with spices. How could Mrs. Baker eat that and not even flinch?

"Are you all right, son?" Mr. Baker asked, concerned.

He couldn't speak so he just nodded his head up and down. He would be fine once he had a drink. He took a swig of his D.T.S. He had been sipping on his soda constantly and it was nearly gone. His throat was still scorching with spice.

"My goodness, his face is turning crimson. Give the boy some water," Mrs. Baker advised.

Poke thrust Peter his measuring cup. Peter took it and began gulping down water. He wasn't getting it all in his mouth; water was splashing everywhere. Poke tried slapping him on the back in case he was choking. With every gulp, his mouth grew hotter. Sweat was building on his brow, and a tear ran down his face.

"What's wrong, Peter?" Mrs. Baker squealed.

Peter tried his hardest to tell them but he could only muster up one word between gulps: "Hot!"

Poke grabbed the Cluck Peter had bitten into and examined it. "It doesn't feel hot."

Peter shook his head furiously.

"Let me see that," Mayor Baker said, holding out his hand. Poke handed the Cluck to him and the mayor held it to his nose.

"It smells very spicy. Is your mouth burning, Peter?" he asked.

Peter nodded, relieved. Mr. Baker handed him the top bun of his burger.

"Eat this; you'll feel better."

By then, Bella had come back to the table to see what the commotion was about. Mrs. Baker explained everything to her while Peter ate the Mayor's bread, which soothed his mouth.

"Oh my." She inspected a Cluck. "I do believe you have mistakenly received a high dose of my special hot spice that is so potent it only requires one dash per recipe. I don't understand how this could have happened, though. I keep the stuff on a separate shelf, and it only goes in specific entrees, and yours was not one of them." She shook her head, perplexed. "I do apologize. This has never happened before. I will make sure you are well taken care of. This meal is on the house, and I will personally get rid of this and make you a fresh batch lickety-split."

Before Peter could say anything, she was off, and she took his rejected meal with her. Peter was beginning to feel better now. His eyes were starting to grow clear, and the fire in his nose and mouth was at a dull burn. He wondered if anyone else had caught sight of the embarrassing scene. It did not appear that way. Wait. His eyes locked on Joe...laughing. A silent laugh where his shoulders raised up and down but no sound came out. He was looking right at Peter. Peter took note of Joe's father, who seemed to be preoccupied with his food and wasn't wondering what his son found so funny. Joe took his fork and pretended to be seasoning his food plentifully with it. Joe's father looked up from his food, and Joe immediately stopped his charade.

Peter was infuriated. He could feel his face turning red all over again. So, that's what Joe was up to when he went in the kitchen earlier. *What a total...*

"Are you feeling better?" Mrs. Baker asked hopefully.

Peter wanted to say something about Joe, but he decided against it.

"I feel much better, thank you," Peter reported even though his pride was squashed.

"I assure you nothing like that has ever happened here before. It must have been an honest mistake," Mr. Baker said.

"I believe you, I really do. I still think this place is totally great." Peter flashed everyone at the table a genuine smile. After all, it wasn't Bella's fault. Peter decided he wouldn't give Joe the satisfaction of looking over at him again.

Everyone at the table let him sample their food, and it was all delicious, better than any restaurant back home. Quite possibly better than his mother's and Nana's home-cooked meals. When Bella brought back his food, it was piled higher than last time, and she even brought him another D.T.S. After the sampling and the bun the mayor had given him to calm his taste buds, he couldn't finish half of his food. Mrs. Baker told him he could take it home for dinner if he wanted, which of course he did.

"Dessert, anyone?" Mr. Baker asked.

"I believe I have a little more room," Mrs.

Baker replied.

"Me, too!" Poke said enthusiastically.

"No thank you," Peter replied honestly. He was stuffed, plus he remembered that their idea of dessert wasn't ever going to be his.

"Well all right, let's go pick something out," the mayor coaxed.

The three dessert eaters got up from the table, and Poke said to Peter, "Come check this out."

They walked up to some washers and dryers along the wall. They weren't actually washers and dryers at all. The washers dispensed cold desserts while the dryers dispensed hot desserts. Looking inside the windows on the door fronts, Peter could see lovely desserts moving slowly round and round on conveyer belts. There were several different kinds. Peter figured they must be coming out from behind the wall. He imagined a rather stout-looking Candonite chef loading the desserts onto the conveyer belt every hour. A panel on the side of each machine contained flashing buttons with numbers zero through nine, and right below them was a set of flashing buttons with a list of the rooms in the restaurant.

Since the group couldn't decide between two different desserts, Mr. Baker proclaimed, "We will just have to get both of them."

"Can I show Peter how it works?" Poke asked eagerly.

"You sure can," the mayor answered, stepping

aside.

First up was the artichoke soufflé, which they found in a dryer. Poke demonstrated how to get it.

"We are sitting at site number eleven in the Laundry Room," Poke informed him. "The site number is on the table where we sat." Peter hadn't noticed. Poke pressed the number one twice and then he pressed the laundry button. The dryer made a buzzing noise as if a load of laundry had finished drying. All the buttons on the machine stopped flashing. Poke opened the door and chose the artichoke soufflé. In Bella's raspy voice, the dryer informed them that a charge of $3.79 would be added to their bill.

"If you pick something up by mistake or change your mind, you put it back and it will not charge you. I think there is a sensor or something that knows how much it weighs," Poke told him.

"That's pretty inventive," Peter stated.

"Give it a try," Poke said, pointing out which dessert Peter should choose. Peter got the second dessert, snow pea and radish pudding, out of the washer the same way. Instead of a buzz, the washer made a dinging noise and said that a charge of $2.99 would be added to their bill.

The looks on their faces as they ate their desserts were the same heavenly smiles of humans consuming their favorite desserts. Peter tried hard not to get grossed out by what they were eating. He reminded himself how he might make them feel.

The take-out box was made of silky smooth paper and laid flat on the table. It was a replica of Bella's restaurant. Bella opened the paper up and there were two slits for a hand to fit through to carry it. She put the food in, fastened it shut, and handed it to Peter. He admired it as he took it and thanked her for her hospitality.

"It was so nice to have met you. I will see you again tonight at the parade." She patted him on the head and continued to wait on other tables.

"She's coming to the parade," Peter repeated to Poke.

"Of course she is. Everyone in Maple Town is," informed Poke.

Peter was starting to get a little nervous about being the honored guest at a parade all for him. The closest he'd come to being the center of attention at a large function was when he played a farmer in a school play a few years back. He wasn't very good at it, either; he kept nibbling on the props, the carrots in his wheelbarrow. He lost track of time, and when he was cued to go on stage, he had a mouthful of carrots and couldn't say his lines clearly. Carrots were spewing out of his mouth all over the stage. Everyone thought it was humorous—everyone except for Peter, of course. He wouldn't eat carrots or hardly look at them for a good half year after that.

"Well, I need to get back to work. Let's get a move on," the mayor commanded.

Everyone rose from the table simultaneously.

Peter then realized he would have to pass Joe on the way out. Ignore him is what he intended to do.

Peter positioned himself beside Poke on the side away from Joe. He heard the Bakers and Poke saying their hellos as they walked on. He knew Joe and his father were next. He felt the anger building inside of him as it had before, and his hand clenched the take-out dome, crushing it slightly. He felt the paper start to crumple, and he stopped. Instead, he clenched his teeth. He heard Joe's obnoxious voice saying hello and the others exchanging their greetings. He looked straight ahead and continued on clenching his teeth until he was safely past them. If he did not see Joe for the rest of his visit in Maple Town, he would be more than happy. He knew it was possible he would run into Joe at the parade. He shuddered to think about it.

The Parade

The festivities would launch at Maple Town Hall. Poke rode along with the Bakers and Peter. Mr. Baker courteously invited Carol Winston to ride with them, but she refused to ride near a rabid human who might strike at any time. If Poke wanted to lose a finger, he was certainly welcome to do so. Peter wasn't too upset that Carol did not join them. He was quite relieved. On the car ride there, no one seemed to be their same sociable selves. No one said anything the whole ride.

When they arrived, cars lined the shiny candy wrapper streets, and many Candonites were hoofing it, heading for the steps of the building. There were so many of them, all glorious and exciting to look at.

Peter was positively nervous now. He could feel his hands turning clammy, his socks getting sweaty, and his stomach filling with butterflies. He gave himself a pep talk and thought there would be no carrots so he wouldn't have to worry about that. He chuckled slightly. However, he did not feel any less nervous. Mrs. Baker must have picked up on how he was feeling.

As they were exiting the car, she whispered to him, "I have faith in you, Peter." Peter smiled back.

He took a deep breath of the sweet-smelling air and relished the moment.

"Will I have to say anything?" he asked Poke.

"You mean like a speech?"

"Yeah."

"No, you just wave."

"Oh."

"Don't worry, I'll be right beside you." Poke nudged him.

Knowing Poke would be with him gave Peter a sense of relief. They made their way up the steps to a luminous violet podium. A huge yellow banner that read "Honoree Parade" hung from the building. Peter knew he was that honoree, and he welled up with pride. He stood a bit taller and lifted his chin slightly as he climbed the steps. He passed by the old gumdrop man he had seen in Old Town the day before. The man was leaning on his crutch, waving at him. Peter waved back. They approached another familiar Candonite. It was Officer O'Bryan. He greeted the mayor, Poke, and Peter with a firm handshake, and kissed Mrs. Baker on the top of her hand as he had done the day before.

"It is nearly time to begin. Unfortunately, I haven't seen our other guest of honor," Officer O'Bryan informed them, looking around the multitude of people. The mayor, Mrs. Baker, and Poke did the same. Peter thought, *Another guest of honor?* He began combing the crowd even though he had no clue who he was looking for.

Moments later, Officer O'Bryan introduced a Candonite woman who resembled a slice of pie. "This is the lady who makes this parade happen, Evelyn Hart, president of the council."

"Nice to meet you," Peter said, shaking her hand, which felt uncannily like pie crust, only none flaked off in his hand.

"A pleasure to meet you as well, Peter," she said. Peter noticed that she blinked an awful lot when she talked. She turned her attention elsewhere. "Where is our other guest? Oh dear. This is cutting it close." She turned her attention back to Peter and said, "Well, I will just have to explain this twice. This is how the festivities will proceed: first the mayor will say the traditional parade day speech. Oh, I do hope that Judge Greg shows up soon. Then you will board the last float of the parade with our other honoree."

Peter was about to ask her who the other honoree might be when she looked beyond him and shrieked with relief, "Oh, there is the judge now! I thought I was going to bust my crust if they did not show up soon." She laughed and snorted at the same time.

Peter saw a rather hefty dark chocolate candy bar Candonite coming quickly through the mass of people up the stairs toward him. *He must be the judge.* He stood and watched as the Candonite man reached the top, turned to look over his shoulder, and stepped aside to reveal the other honoree. Peter saw a face he was oh so familiar with and couldn't contain his happiness. It was...Lina. *But how is that possible?* She was also overjoyed to see him. He ran up to her and gave her the biggest hug he had given anyone in a while.

"Okay, okay, enough of this mushy gushy stuff," she said as Peter released her. He was a tad embarrassed but quickly gathered himself.

Peter rattled off in rapid-fire succession, "I am so glad to see you. I thought no one would believe me when I told them about this place. Now that you are here...well, they have to! How about that? I believe Nana was here too when she was younger. How did you get here? Was it the same way I did? How long have you been here?"

"Calm down, Peter. I want to know the same things about you," Lina interrupted. "But, first, let me introduce someone. I don't want to be rude." She turned to the robust candy bar Candonite and said, "This is Judge Greg. I have been staying with him and his family since yesterday."

"Hello, young man," the judge said in an exceptionally deep voice that matched his stature.

"Hello," Peter responded.

Evelyn Hart had made her way over to them and said hurriedly, "We have no time to chat. We must get this show on the road." Pleased with herself, she laughed and snorted again, saying, "We *really* do need to get this show on the road."

Judge Greg escorted Peter and Lina to the spots where they would stand during the ceremony.

Peter was super-excited and nervous at the same time. Lina was there, so it made the experience even more extraordinary. The noises of the crowd quieted when Mayor Baker approached the podium. Out of respect for the mayor and the judge, Lina and Peter were very quiet even though they wanted to talk about their adventures.

"Good people of Maple Town, thank you for joining us this evening. We have in our midst two very fine humans. We have gathered to honor them tonight. My wife and I have had the pleasure of young Peter Fischer staying with us." He turned toward Peter and motioned for him to move forward. Peter did so hesitantly and waved at the mass of Candonites. His spirit soared as the crowd cheered back. What had he done to deserve such treatment? He did not know, but he sure was soaking it up. He waved once more, and the crowd roared again. He stepped back toward Lina, who was smiling proudly.

Mayor Baker continued, "At this time, I would like to introduce you to a wonderful girl named Lina Young. Judge Greg and his family have had the pleasure to spend time with her."

The mayor turned toward Lina and made the same motions to her. She stepped forward and waved as Peter had before, only she didn't attempt the second wave. She returned to stand next to Peter. She was smiling bigger than he had ever seen her smile. He was so glad to be sharing this moment with her. She really was a great friend.

"Now, I would like to ask that you would find it in your hearts to agree with me on this following statement. I understand that these children have come to us by doing wrong...by Bellyache." At hearing this, Peter's stomach dropped, his spirits plummeted. He looked at Lina in dismay. She looked as if she might want to hide behind Judge Greg. They shared the same shame. They had lied, disobeyed their loved ones, and gorged themselves loony. "But I believe they have learned their lesson!" The crowd roared again in confident agreement. This made the children breathe sighs of relief.

Mayor Baker stepped aside, and Evelyn Hart took the podium. "At this time, I'd like to ask the float riders to please man your floats. The parade will begin shortly. Also, the Student Union will be selling desserts on the north lawn to help fund their next trip to Honeyville and to assist with the upkeep of our fabulous parade floats. Thank you, and good evening." She then scuttled over to Peter and Lina. "Come, children, come with me." The Bakers, Judge Greg, and Poke followed. The rest of the crowd turned toward the streets, and some headed toward the north lawn. They were preparing to watch the parade.

Poke came alongside Peter, and he introduced him to Lina. "This is Poke. He is visiting his aunt who lives next door to the Bakers." Carol Winston crept into Peter's mind as he spoke, and he shook her out of it as swiftly as he could.

"Hi. I have to say, I totally love your town. I wish we could stay longer. Don't you, Peter?" she said enthusiastically.

"Heck yeah!" Peter replied.

"So what happened, anyway? How did you get here?" Lina inquired.

Peter explained to her how he had found himself standing next to her now. He was more interested in finding out how she was there.

When they reached the back entrance of the town hall, they heard voices behind the exit door. Evelyn Hart gave them directions, "Please wait here. I need to make sure everything is in order before we get started. Order is absolutely essential for a perfect parade." Then she stepped out.

While they waited, Lina shared her story of how she came to find herself in this wondrous place. She reminded Peter of how her dad had told her that the candy she bought at Papa's Sweet Shop had to last all week. That night after dinner, she went to her room and began reading an article in a sports magazine. There was a picture of famous baseball players, one of whom was holding a candy bar. She started craving her candy. She went to the kitchen drawer where she had stashed it and couldn't decide what she wanted, so she took the whole lot upstairs with her. Once she made her choice, she intended to bring the rest back downstairs. Instead, she started tossing piece after piece into her mouth while she read. The next thing she knew, there was nothing to put back. She told of how she started feeling icky and laid her head down on her desk. The next thing she remembered, she had fallen asleep and woke up to an image of a brown package on her computer screen floating around. It had gleaming red letters reading "Special Delivery." She told of how it looked as though it were popping off the screen. The overwhelming urge to touch it was unbearable.

"The rest of the story you already know, Peter," she concluded.

They were amazed at how similar their stories were, and they agreed they would never stuff themselves silly like that again. They both also admitted to feeling bad about what they had done.

"Our parents must be worried sick about us," Lina stated.

Until then, Peter hadn't thought of it. Everyone was probably freaking out! How selfish he had been to not even think of how his family must be feeling. He certainly hoped they weren't blaming his grandpa for anything. He began to feel overcome with guilt.

"Worried sick," Peter repeated in a whisper.

"I am sure everything will be just fine. You are good children who made a mistake. Mistakes are worth forgiveness when you truly mean you're sorry," Mrs. Baker said in a sweet, soothing voice.

This made them feel better. Just then, the back door flung open and Evelyn came in carrying two golden medallions with royal blue ribbons tied to them. They were beautiful, and they shined so brightly that everyone had to squint to get a good look at them. Peter hoped one was for him.

"These are for you two." Evelyn hesitated for a moment and stared at the children before putting the medallions around Lina and Peter's necks. "Wear them with pride, children." There was a hint of apprehension in her voice. "They are one hundred years old and made by our beloved ancestors."

"Thank you," they said in unison.

They both admired their exquisite gifts. They were exactly alike. Inscribed on each medallion were the words "Forgive" on the front and "Free" on the back. On the front were three hills and three castles that adorned their tops. Carved pictures of a human boy and girl were on the back.

"I wonder who they were," Lina said, barely audible.

The children stared at their medallions.

Evelyn Hart's voice broke the silence. "Let's get this baby started!" she said as she flailed her arms and opened the door to lead them out.

The floats were impressive and familiar.

"Look," Peter said excitedly to Lina, "the Statue of Liberty!"

"Over there, Peter, it's Mount Rushmore!"

Peter and Lina recited the recognizable features of the floats.

"Empire State Building!"

"The Eiffel Tower!"

"The Great Sphinx!"

"The Great Wall of China!"

"The Leaning Tower of Pisa!"

They saw one very familiar place at the same time and said, "Disney World!" They both laughed. There were plenty of other famous places amidst the floats as well. It was a tribute to the world Peter and Lina were from. Some of the floats were hovering; others were still on the ground. There were twelve in total, all manned by Candonites. Evelyn Hart led them to their float, the last one in the line.

"Isn't it incredible here?" Lina stated to Peter.

"Yeah, I wish we didn't have to go so soon," Peter confessed.

"Me, too!"

Their float was the one that had Disney World and several other famous places on it. They admitted it was the one they wanted to ride on the most. When they reached the float, they saw that no one was on it. Evelyn Hart pressed her foot down on an emerald green button on the side of the float and out came steps to allow them to climb up.

"All aboard!" Evelyn called and snorted with delight at her comment once again.

The children boarded first, and behind them the Bakers clutched hands and exchanged a look of sorrow that the children did not see. The Bakers regained control of their feelings and displayed gracious smiles upon boarding the float. When they were all on board, Evelyn Hart pushed the emerald button again, and the steps disappeared back into the float.

"Good luck, and I wish you all well!" Evelyn Hart called. She then turned swiftly and scuttled away with her hands together and her head down. The children thought she must be worried about the parade going smoothly.

In front of the float, there was a steering wheel with some buttons in the middle. Mayor Baker stepped up to the wheel. The children positioned themselves together toward the center of the float, and Mrs. Baker kept near her husband. Judge Greg lingered at the back of the float. Moments later, there was a loud, explosive cannon sound, and the parade was on its way.

Peter and Lina felt giant butterflies in their stomachs as soon as the float began to move.

"What do you think the medallions mean, Peter?" Lina asked, mystified.

Peter was too busy concentrating on how he was going to wave at the crowd. He said, "I think it means they forgave us for gorging ourselves silly with things resembling the Candonites before we arrived in Maple Town."

"What about the 'free' part?"

Annoyed because he could see some adoring fans and he wanted to give them his full attention, he said, "I guess it means that even though we didn't do right in how we got here, we were forgiven and we get to roam around freely, instead of being thrown in the slammer or something."

"Oh, I suppose that is a possibility," Lina replied, not impressed with his explanation.

"Come on, Lina, wave at the good people," Peter advised.

Lina saw that everyone on the float was waving vigorously, and she didn't want to disappoint. She joined in, forgetting about the medallions for now. The crowd was cheering them on. It was one of the best feelings the children had ever felt. Peter noticed a Candonite that looked a bit like Joe holding a peppermint cat. She was much older than Joe's father. Her head was bowed, and she was stroking the peppermint cat. Perhaps it was the same peppermint cat that Peter had seen yesterday. What's this? Was she crying? The float had passed her and she was out of his range of view. Peter tried to catch another glimpse in vain; she had vanished. He felt a little uneasy at what he had just seen and convinced himself she probably hadn't been crying. He focused his attention back to enjoying the crowd.

He hadn't even pushed the woman out of his head when Lina said something disturbing. "I just saw a Candonite man crying. He was standing there crying." She pointed back in the direction of where she had seen him, and Peter hurried to look but saw no one crying.

Poke spoke up and shifted their attention to the sky. "Look up. That is for you two!"

The mayor and the Mrs. looked back to make

sure the children were paying attention. Little marshmallow birds were flying lightning fast through the sky.

"What are they doing?" Lina asked, amazed.

"You'll see," Poke answered.

They gazed toward the sky and watched as the little birds made their first symbol. It was a human girl and a boy, symbolic of Lina and Peter. As fast as the symbol appeared, it was gone. Soon the elegant birds formed a massive heart pulsing in the sky. And they spread their wings in sync, in and out, with every heartbeat. One by one, the birds flew out of the heart shape and speedily created their next formation. The children couldn't quite make out what they were forming; it didn't really look like anything.

"I think they are spelling something," Peter observed.

"I think you're right," Lina said.

Soon the letters were complete and the birds had spelled "Free." As swiftly as they spelled it, they flew off in different directions.

"What does it mean?" Lina asked Poke.

"I don't know. The birds create as they feel led. It is different every time we have human visitors. Only you and Peter can figure out what it means," Poke answered.

Mayor Baker looked over his shoulder at the children, and with a straight face confirmed, "Peter and Lina, you have to figure out what it means on your own."

Peter and Lina looked at each other, dumb-founded. Then Lina spoke confidently, "I'm sure we can figure it out together, Peter."

"Of course we will, but first we get back to waving."

They continued through the candy wrapper streets, waving and taking in the splendid cheers. Peter and Lina were thoroughly enjoying themselves, when out of the crowd Carol Winston emerged. She was making such an awful scene. Her finger was pointing viciously in the direction of Peter and Lina. Her voice was strong and fierce and was becoming more audible as they neared.

"They won't help them! They'll go home! Filthy, cowardly creatures!" she kept repeating, getting louder and louder as they approached.

Peter and Lina were horrified. For that matter, so was everyone on the float. Poke felt somewhat responsible for her actions because she was his aunt.

"Ignore my aunt; she doesn't know any better," Poke insisted.

"Pay her no mind, children," Judge Greg's deep voice advised from behind.

Officer O'Bryan suddenly appeared from the thick crowd. He took Carol Winston by the arm and escorted her away. Carol Winston didn't go silently.

"She doesn't like us very much," Lina stated.

"She doesn't understand humans at all," Poke explained.

The floats in front continued on. But Peter and Lina's float had its own agenda. It veered to the right as the other floats followed the street left. It was hovering over the grass now and heading steadily up the blue-green hill.

The Choice

"Where are we going?" Lina asked.

"It's nearly time to say our farewells, dears," Mrs. Baker said kindly. She looked very sad.

"We're on our way home," Lina told Peter; her voice was bittersweet.

Peter turned to Poke, who tried to look cheery even though Peter could tell he was a bit disappointed. They had become good friends in such a short time.

"We knew this time was coming, but it still gets ya, you know?" Poke confessed to Peter.

"I know," Peter said empathetically. He felt the same way.

Peter saw the same trees he had seen the day before, the pointing trees. There was something different about these trees, though. He was sure it was the same path he followed to get to Maple Town. These trees were pointing away from Maple Town, in the direction they were headed.

"This looks like the path I took to get to Maple Town," Lina stated.

"I'm pretty sure it's the same one I took, too," Peter said.

"Strange," Lina replied.

Shortly after they had gotten over the hill, they noticed three figures in the distance.

"I wonder who they are," Lina said softly.

"Probably some Candonites to see us off," Peter suggested.

Just then, they noticed Mrs. Baker clasp her hand over her mouth and the mayor drop his head and shake it slowly. Peter looked at Lina and she shrugged.

As they approached, Peter recognized one of the figures. It was Joe's father. Peter looked around for Joe. Thank goodness he wasn't there. He did not recognize the others. As they grew closer, Peter could see their faces were glum.

"Those are Angela's parents; Angela is the girl who brought me to the judge's house," Lina informed Peter.

Peter studied Angela's parents and determined that they were both Candonites of the cookie race. They looked similar except the wife had rainbow-colored chips.

"Angela is as dreadful as can be," Lina whispered to Peter.

"That is Joe's father; Joe is the boy who brought me to the mayor's." Peter lowered his voice, "and Joe has got to be worse than Angela."

"I doubt that."

"I wonder why they look so sad," Peter inquired to everyone. No one answered.

The float was right beside them now.

"Look there," Peter said as he spotted something familiar. "It's the package!"

The package was lying on the ground, slightly opened, marked with the same red "Special Delivery."

"I guess that's how we get home," Lina said.

"You got it," Mayor Baker confirmed.

"Oh, I'm not ready to go home yet," Lina whined.

"Me neither," Peter confessed.

As the float came to a stop, Mayor Baker pressed a ruby button on the steering wheel, and the steps of the float lowered. Everyone exited the float. They approached the three Candonites huddled together, and Mayor Baker told the others to please gather around. They did as they were told. Peter gave a quick look at the package sitting off to the side. They could see the faces of the three closely now, and they looked terribly worried. This made Peter and Lina very nervous. Peter and Lina exchanged glances and could see the other's concern. Joe's dad and Angela's dad each held up a gray pebble in the palm of their hands. The pebbles were lying on small charcoal mesh bags.

Mayor Baker cleared his throat. "Peter and Lina, I have something important to tell you. Listen very carefully." The tone of his voice was alarmingly serious. The children edged closer to be sure to not miss a word. Mayor Baker continued, "This is where your visit with us may end or where your new journey may begin. You have only to touch the special delivery package you came here in and speak these words: 'Free to go home.' Repeat it back to me, please; I want to be sure you know exactly what must be said."

Peter and Lina obeyed. "Free to go home."

The mayor went on, "There is something else I regret to inform you of..." There was an earsplitting screech, and Angela's mother fell toward the ground, partially held up by her husband. She had fainted, and her husband and Joe's father were tending to her as she came to.

"She'll be fine. Please go on, mayor." Angela's father's voice was weak.

"It's Joe and Angela. They have vanished. And you, Peter and Lina, are the only ones who can save them. You see, we do not have the capability. Their behavior toward you was intolerable. You are the only ones who have the choice to save them."

The children's feelings were mixed. Why should they care? *Oh, that is terrible!* Between the two of them, they honestly did not know how to respond.

"What do you mean we have to save them?" Peter asked, concerned.

Mayor Baker pointed over their heads. "They are there."

Everyone's eyes followed in the direction the mayor was pointing.

"Where? There's nothing that way but a bunch of grass and more of those pointing trees," Lina observed.

Out of nowhere, the ground beneath them began to rumble and the trees shook violently, their pointing branches swaying up and down. Everyone was frightened.

"I don't know anything more. We must be going," Mayor Baker urged, composing himself.

"We must say our good-byes, dears," Mrs. Baker said, rushed.

Mayor and Mrs. Baker reached for Lina and Peter to give each of them a warm, quick embrace. Peter could see a tear in Mrs. Baker's eye and it made him sad. The good-byes were happening so fast that Peter couldn't think of what to say. Not to mention the fact that the Candonites were counting on him to be a superhero. The closest he ever came to being a hero was...well, never.

"Be safe, children, and as I told you before, Peter, I have faith in you," Mrs. Baker said.

"It was grand to have met you both...such an honor," Mayor Baker added sincerely.

Mayor Baker began hurriedly escorting the parents toward the float. Angela's mom had regained her strength and pleaded with Peter and Lina for a moment. "Please, please, help my child!" Her husband stopped her before she could say anymore and solemnly led her away.

Poke lingered with Lina and Peter as the others boarded the float. He spoke from the heart. "Sorry I can't help you out with your situation. I don't really know anything. I want you to know that I really had a great time hanging out, and at risk of sounding corny, I'm gonna miss having you around."

Peter also risked sounding corny. "I'm gonna miss hanging out, too."

"Oh just hug already!" Lina shoved Peter forward.

They gave each other a speedy guy hug, and then Poke was off to join the others, all of whom looked rather glum. Peter and Lina watched as the float descended toward Maple Town.

Peter was genuinely going to miss them. Despite the fact he had met them only the day before, he felt as though he had known them much longer. Once the float was out of sight, Peter's thoughts shifted back to the task before them.

Lina's voice sounded almost deafening in the gloomy silence. "What are you waiting for, Peter? Let's get going."

Peter agreed with Lina. What was he waiting for?

Peter turned around to walk in the direction which the mayor had pointed to earlier. He really couldn't stand Joe, and from what Lina had said about Angela, she was no saint, but they were, after all, someone's children, and Joe was Bella's godson. And Mr. Baker had said Lina and Peter were their only hope.

"Hey, where do you think you're going?" Lina called out.

Peter was surprised her voice was distant. He figured she was right behind him. He swung around to see what was up.

"Aren't you coming?" Peter inquired.

"Coming where? There isn't anything that way for a far stretch. The only place I am going is home!" Lina said, moving toward the special package.

Peter hurried after her. "Wait, what about Joe and Angela?"

Lina spat back, "What about them?"

"We can't just leave them there."

"Leave them where? And yes we can."

Peter tried to talk some sense into her. "You heard Mayor Baker. We are their only chance!"

"Angela is a wicked little girl, and from what I gather from you about Joe, he is no Mr. Nice Guy either. Besides, what could possibly be so bad? There isn't anything unpleasant except for them in this whole magnificent place," Lina spoke, irritated.

"But..."

"But nothing," Lina said. "I want to go home. I bet my family is worried sick about me. My mom probably called the police, my dad is probably searching the neighborhood inch by inch, and my brother has probably moved his things into my room and is jumping for joy on my bed as we speak!" She put her hands on the red letters of the package. The letters began to faintly glow.

Her voice was so demanding. Peter moved to put his hands on the package, too. When he touched it, the letters brightened.

"Okay then, we only need to say the magic words together. Ready?" She stared, searching for an answer.

"Ready," Peter said reluctantly.

"Say it with me now," Lina commanded.

Together they spoke aloud, "Free to go..."

"*Noooooo!*" Peter cried with stunning force as he yanked his arms away from the package. He blinked long and hard, expecting Lina to be gone when his eyes opened. But she wasn't, her face staring back at his with both hands on her hips.

She spoke softly. "I couldn't do it. I stopped speaking after saying, 'Free.' I wanted to say the whole thing, but my mouth wouldn't do it. I guess I have to admit, I am a little scared. Saving others is a big responsibility, and it's not like we got a lot of information on the situation." Her face turned serious. "If you tell anyone I said I was scared, I'll knock you for a loop!" She made a fist with her right hand.

Peter had never known Lina to be afraid of anything. She wasn't afraid of spiders, older menacing boys, not even scary movies. Under the circumstances, though, he understood. He nodded at her to let her know that it would be their secret.

"I'm sure glad you stuck around," Peter admitted.

"Hey, I wouldn't want you to get all the credit for saving those lugheads." She smiled.

"Besides," Peter stated, looking at the shiny medallion, "these are pictures of the two of us."

"You're right. Lead us on our quest, captain."

"I'm not leading us anywhere." Peter took Lina's hand; it was clammy, and he squeezed it tight. "We do it together...we do it as a team."

"Fine, but holding my hand does not change our relationship in any way. I'll pound you into mud if you try anything else!" she warned. Peter knew she was serious. He wasn't planning on it. He was plainly frightened of what might lie ahead; they both were.

The Stench

Peter and Lina took extremely deep breaths, gave each other a look of encouragement, and together they moved toward the unknown. The blue-green grass seemed a little grayer now, and the sun wasn't shining as brightly.

Peter started to comment on his observation when, alarmingly, he felt out of breath. He felt Lina squeeze his hand hard in a death grip. He shut his eyes and gasped for air. He reopened them and found gloom and a vast land of gray, nothing familiar. No blue-green grass, no chirping marshmallow birds, not even a gummy worm...only silence. He felt the life sucking out of him and gasped once more, filling his lungs triumphantly with a thick breath...thick with stench. He started to gag and almost wished he still couldn't breathe as his eyes watered in reaction to the pungent smell. It was one of the worst smells that had ever entered his nose, right up there with the time he had forgotten to take out the trash that contained tuna casserole before going on a two-week family vacation. He placed his right arm over his nose and remembered Lina, her grip much looser now. Was she all right? He hadn't heard her gasp.

Peter positioned himself in front of Lina, never

letting her hand go. To Peter's horror, she looked a shade of faint purple. *She can't breathe!* he thought.

"Disgusting, it smells like my brother's sneakers here!" Lina gasped.

"You're all right!" Peter exclaimed, pulling his arm away from his nose and grabbing Lina's available hand with his. He was pretty sure he looked like a cheerleader the way he jumped up and down, holding her hands. But he did not care. His best friend was all right, and he wouldn't have to trek through this dreadful place without her. Best friend—Peter had never thought about it before, but it was true. His best friend was a girl...Lina.

"You can let go of my hands now. I need them to cover my nose," she said seriously yet playfully, squishing up her face with disgust. Peter let them go.

"What do you think that smell is, Peter?"

"I don't know, and I'd rather not think about it. All I do know is the sooner we get to looking for Joe and Angela, the sooner we get out of here and back to some fresh, sweet-smelling air and sunshine," Peter stated.

"Yeah, I can't wait to get..." Lina's eyes fixed on something in the distance. She finished her sentence under her breath, "out of here."

Peter, curious and worried, turned around to see what she was staring at. There were three gigantic and eerie, grand, dark castles, each sitting atop its own enormous hill.

"They look painfully far away," Lina admitted.

Peter and Lina both looked back the way they had come and saw that it looked no different from where they were; the same gray grass stretched as far as their eyes could see. They focused back on the castles.

"We can't possibly go to all three castles. That would take forever. How will we know which one to go to or even if going to them is what we should do?" Peter whined.

"Look," Lina pointed at Peter's chest. "Your medallion."

Peter observed his medallion; it was lit up with a golden glow.

"It started glowing when you said 'castles.' It's as if it liked that idea."

"Your medallion, it's glowing now, too." Peter gave a nod of approval.

"Well, that is that; we are going to those castles," Lina commanded.

With their medallions' reassurance, Peter and Lina headed toward the shadowy castles, trying not to mind the awful smell. As they approached the castles, their surroundings grew dimmer. The grass appeared dark gray, almost black, and so did the few trees that were scattered about.

Peter slowed in his tracks. "Listen."

Lina answered abruptly. "I don't hear anything."

"Neither do I," he confirmed.

The dead silence sent shivers down both their

spines. They continued forward, more cautiously. The grass beneath their feet had disappeared and turned into dirt and gravel. They came upon a narrow crossing that branched into three paths. Each of the paths led toward a different castle.

"Great, now what?" Lina moaned.

"I don't know."

They stood there, taking in the sight of the three uninviting castles before them.

"They're creepy. I don't like the idea of having to go inside," Lina said.

"Me, neither," Peter responded, "but we have to, for Joe and Angela and their parents. Besides, I don't want that mean ol' Carol Winston strutting around, chanting how she knew we wouldn't help them!"

"The castles all look the same, dark with hardly any light coming from them. This is like something out of a scary movie," Lina said, spooked.

"Except it isn't...it is real life."

Lina sank down on a large rock. "I am pooped. Look how much farther we have to go, and the smell isn't getting any better, either."

"I am tired, too, but the sooner we find those two, the sooner we can go home and see our families."

"True. I can't wait to tell them about all this!" Lina exclaimed, springing up from the rock. "Let's ask the medallions."

"What?" Peter looked surprised.

"Come on, Peter, like we did before when we said, 'castles,' and the medallions glowed. So maybe we could sort of ask them which one to go to." She raised her shoulders and gave a little shrug.

"It's worth a shot, I guess. Should we go to the castle on the left?" The two fixed their eyes on the medallions but nothing happened. Peter looked up at Lina, and she gave him the "go ahead; try again" look his mother would give him when he couldn't get a homework problem correct the first try. "Should we go to the castle in the middle?" Still the medallions did nothing. The children were beginning to think the medallions weren't going to reply. Raising his hand, Peter pointed firmly at the last castle and asked more boldly, "Should we go the castle on the right?"

The two stared hopefully at the medallions. They both had been holding their breath and let out the air as their medallions started glowing. They rejoiced, giving each other high fives.

"I knew it had to work!" Lina sing-songed.

Peter was relieved to hear a cheerful pitch in her voice. There was still hope.

"Let's get this party started!" Peter joked.

They both laughed nervously as they moved cautiously towards the medallions' choice. The air grew frosty as they approached the castle.

"It's closer than we thought it was and smaller than it looked from far away," Lina stated.

"Yeah, it is," Peter agreed.

The dark gray castle showed little life except

for the occasional flicker of light. There were three towers. The center one was taller than the others. More light flickered from that tower than from any other room in the castle. They reached the massive castle doors, which looked an ill fit for the small-sized castle. The entire castle was composed of tiny gray pebbles.

"It must have taken forever to build!" Peter observed, touching his finger to a single gray stone.

"Jeez, it's really cold right here," Lina whined through chattering teeth.

"And really quiet, too."

As if something was disturbed by what they said, there was a rustle in a tall gray bush behind them. Startled, the children jumped into the castle doors, and they responded with a crackling thud. The crackling turned into a cracking noise that continued to escalate.

Peter wrapped his arm around Lina's shoulders and dove forward into the gritty dirt and grass. "It's coming down!"

They hit the ground hard and shielded their faces. They were engulfed by puffs of dirt and smoke and the sounds of thousands of pebbles falling to the ground behind them. The ruckus lasted for a half minute, and it was that long before they were able to look back at the castle. Rubble coated the ground where the giant door had stood just moments before. In the midst of it all there was a thin, clear path leading inside the castle.

The bush rustled again and from it darted a tiny dark blur. A mouse.

"That was a rush!" Lina exclaimed, dusting off her knees.

"Well, I guess we don't have to knock," Peter said sarcastically, catching his breath.

"True," Lina said, walking slowly toward the path. "You coming?" she said without looking back at Peter.

"Of course I am," Peter stated with a newfound sense of curiosity. He shuffled toward her, taking in the scene. "I should go first," he said boldly, "in case it is dangerous."

She gave him the "you have got to be kidding" look. He had seen that look from her once before on Halloween, when they were about to ring Old Man Saget's doorbell and run as punishment for him not giving out candy again that year. Peter suggested that he do it because it might be too dangerous. Lina rang the doorbell.

Now she continued forward cautiously, in front.

Forgiveness

Once inside, it was frightfully cold and smelled just as unpleasant. Peter looked over at Lina, who was crossing her arms, rubbing them. Together they analyzed the mostly empty grand room. There was an immense rumble from behind them, and the children jerked around. They were hearing the same noises as before entering: cracking sounds.

Oh spam! thought Peter.

"Not again!" Lina crouched down to protect herself. Peter thought that wasn't a bad idea and did the same.

Lina shielded her face with open fingers so she could still see what was going on. Peter did not bother shielding his face; he realized right away what was going on.

"The door's rebuilding itself," Peter said.

Lina put her hands down and watched intently as the giant door began to take form again. Everything that had fallen was returning to its rightful place. Every pebble and every speck of dust swirled upward, a cloudy mass of dark gray flowing toward the ceiling. The cracking turned into creaking, and then, as quickly as it started, it was dead silent, except for the heavy breathing of the children.

"Wow, that was amazing." Lina said.

They rose to their feet to find the room darker without the extra light coming in from outside. Only one tiny spherical window let in dim light from high above. Except for the two of them, the vast room was empty: no chairs, no couches, not even a side table.

"We wouldn't find this place on the cover of one of my mother's home magazines," Lina cracked, shivering. "Could you imagine?"

"No way!" Peter remarked, imagining Lina's mother relaxing at home, sipping her tea, turning the pages of her magazine to see "Ghastly Pebble Castle." Then the tea cup goes crashing down.

"She'd be cleaning that up for a while," he said out loud.

"Cleaning what?"

"Oh, nothing," he answered.

"Well, I don't want to be in here any longer than we have to, so let's get down to business, or should I say up to business?" Lina pointed toward a set of stone stairs. Their eyes followed the staircase. It wound around the room in a colossal swirl.

"There doesn't seem to be anyone or anything down here, but we should look around first to make sure."

"Lead the way, Sherlock."

Peter led Lina silently around the entire room. They found no one and no thing, as they suspected.

"This place is strange," Lina broke the silence.

"No kidding, it gives me the creeps."

"Well, Nancy Drew, shall we see where those stairs take us?" Lina tried to lighten the mood.

Peter gave her a look of disapproval. He did not like being called a girl. "Oh, go on, lead the way, Scooby." She giggled playfully.

A smile cracked from his lips, and he led the way to the steps. The staircase was sparingly lit by the lone window above. He took a breath and put his right foot on the first step.

"Wait, Peter," Lina said quietly. "We are about to climb all these stairs and we don't even know what is up there."

They both looked at their medallions for reassurance. The medallions didn't so much as flicker.

Peter paused for a moment and called out, "Hello, anyone up there?" His words fell flat. There was no echo; it was as if his words did not travel more than a few feet in front of him. Peter and Lina looked at each other, stupefied. The familiar joyfulness of Maple Town seemed so far away now.

"We have to at least take a look. We can't turn back now," Peter said strongly.

"I'm scared. I don't think I..." Her thoughts flashed back to seeing Carol Winston's distorted face in the crowd, screaming. Lina started fuming as she heard those words repeated in her head. "We're going up these stairs! No one's going to tell me what I am going to do!" She grabbed Peter's arm firmly and pulled him up the first few steps.

A great wind came from beneath their feet and lifted them round and round the staircase in the flash of an eye, to the door at the very top of the tower. Then it stopped. The children's hearts were racing, and their faces looked bewildered.

"Some service," Lina spoke excitedly. "We'd have been climbing those stairs all day if that...whatever that was hadn't given us a lift."

"That was some ride," Peter said, looking beneath their feet as if to find some sort of evidence of what had just happened.

The children noticed the door now, tall and wide. It had a handle made of the same pebbles that formed the entire castle. The children half expected it to crumble to the ground as the one before had. They stood there waiting. Nothing.

"I think we better open it," Peter announced, looking at the medallions for some clarity.

Lina noticed, "I think they might be broken."

"Or maybe it is time we do it on our own," Peter responded.

"Maybe, or maybe we are making the wrong choice," Lina shrugged. "There is only one way to find out."

Peter and Lina grabbed the pebbled handle together and tugged. It easily opened. They were hit immediately by the thickened, pungent, icy air.

Lina gagged. "Oh, it's terrible, way worse than my brother's sneakers!"

"It's so cold; I can see your breath." Peter

fanned his nose.

"Look, up there." Lina pointed, and Peter's eyes followed.

There, high above them, hanging from the ceiling in golden cages, were Joe and Angela. Peter was seeing Angela for the first time. She looked like a mini version of her mother, rainbow chips and all. They both leapt in the direction of Peter and Lina and were very excited and relieved to see them. Their mouths were moving, but Peter and Lina couldn't hear anything.

"The cages must be made of glass," Peter concluded.

"That's a change in Angela's attitude. The last time I saw her, she was spitting sunflower seeds in my hair. Who would have thought she would be happy to see me," Lina huffed, with one hand on her hip. "Although I do kinda feel sorry for her, hanging up there hopelessly like that." Lina's body language softened.

The children entered the tower and took a glance around. There was nothing except for the two hanging cages. They continued to move toward the golden cages. The only light coming from the tower was from the cages themselves.

"How did they get up there?" Peter wondered.

"Better yet, how do we get them down?" Lina replied.

Peter and Lina gazed up at the desperate-looking children. Both of them were on their knees so they could get a better look at what Peter and Lina were doing. Lina and Peter both waved up at the Candonite children. Angela and Joe returned weak waves.

"What are they doing now?" Lina questioned.

"Looks like they are pointing."

"At what? There is nothing there. Just the wall. Wait a minute, now they are pointing at that wall over there. What are they doing?" Lina seemed annoyed.

"Maybe they are trying to tell us something," Peter suggested.

"Or maybe they have just gone mad." Lina gave attitude.

"Let's check it out." Peter walked toward the first wall Joe and Angela had pointed to.

"Check what out?" Lina asked.

Peter ignored her and continued to walk toward the wall, turning back to take one more look at the Candonite children. They seemed intent on what he was doing and continued to point vigorously toward the wall. Lina followed close behind him. Peter felt a sudden overwhelming cautious feeling and abruptly stopped. Lina walked right into him.

"Hey, what's the matter?" Lina whispered, looking at Peter's intense eyes.

"I don't know; probably nothing," he responded, not wanting to worry her, although he wondered if she felt the eeriness, too.

She did feel it. She sensed that Peter shared

her feeling. "Step aside, mister. I'm going to prove to you that they are nuts and there is nothing here." She shoved past him and walked straight up to the pebbled wall. She touched it, pushed it, rolled her fingers over some of the pebbles, and examined it closely. "Nothing but millions of pebbles here, as I suspected."

Peter looked back up at Joe and Angela. They both had their eyes covered with their hands, the way someone would if they were about to see a scary part in a movie.

"What is the matter with those two?" Lina puzzled.

Peter walked next to Lina, who was now leaning on the wall with her arms crossed. "Have a look for yourself. You won't find anything."

She was right. He did nose around and found nothing, except for the same lingering pungent smell, which seemed to be even worse. His stomach turned.

"We need to figure out how to get those two out of here fast. I think I am going to be sick." Lina held her stomach.

Above Lina's left shoulder, two deep dark eyes, yellow where the whites of the eyes should be, appeared and vanished back into the wall before anyone had a chance to notice.

Peter and Lina returned to the cages, where they observed Angela and Joe still looking around at the walls.

"They must be frightened that this will be

what they will stare at for the rest of their lives if we don't save them. Dark, gloomy, pebbled walls. I don't blame them at all for being worried. I'm not convinced we will find a way to get them out. I know they were terribly mean to us, but they don't deserve this," Lina said honestly.

"Let's continue looking; maybe we are missing something," Peter suggested.

"Looking at what? We checked. The walls look the same all the way around, and there is nothing on the floor except for thousands of those pebbles."

Peter's mind flashed to Mrs. Baker's sweet voice saying, "I have faith in you."

"We will get them down and safely home. I have enough faith for the both of us," Peter stated, unwavering.

"I am with you, Peter."

They took a step back and peered up at the Candonite children.

Peter did not know if the children could hear them, but he felt it necessary to encourage them. "We are going to get you out!" he said with big hand movements, trying to express what he was saying.

Angela and Joe's faces expressed immense shame. They approached the glass of their cages, put their hands up to it, and mouthed the words, "I'm sorry." They truly looked genuine in their gestures.

"I really think they are sorry, and not just because they want us to save them. They have no more a clue than we do about how to get them down," Lina observed.

"It's all right. I forgive you!" Peter shouted. He looked over at Lina.

She searched her feelings and shouted in the same fashion as Peter, "I forgive you, too!"

Angela and Joe looked relieved and thankful for Peter and Lina's forgiveness. All four children exchanged smiles.

At that moment, Peter and Lina noticed two small cracks in the floor beneath the cages begin to glow.

"What do you suppose it is?" Peter asked.

Lina did not answer because she did not know.

"They're doing it again." Peter sounded enthusiastic.

Lina looked up toward Angela and Joe, who were staring back at them. "They are not doing anything," Lina said.

"Not them," Peter replied. "The medallions...they are glowing."

Lina swung her head around to fix her eyes on them. "What does it mean?"

Peter walked toward the light coming from the crack beneath Joe; Lina followed. Peter knelt down in front of one of the cracks and examined it. He could make out the form of the crack, and he traced it with his finger and stuck it in to measure. He couldn't quite touch the bottom.

"What are you doing?" Lina asked.

"I don't believe it is a crack at all." He took his medallion off. "More like a slot." Lina watched Peter closely. She was beginning to think he was on to something.

"Forgiveness will set you free," Peter said, barely above a whisper. He placed it in the slot on the floor. It fit perfectly, just like a quarter into an arcade game. With a deep breath, he let the medallion go, and it disappeared, with the ribbon flapping down into the floor. The light that shone from both the slot and the medallion was abruptly gone.

"You broke it!" exclaimed Lina.

Noise like running water was coming from above. Something was happening to Joe's cage. Peter got up from the floor and stepped back to get a better look. Lina backed up, too. Joe looked unnerved. The glass around him appeared to be steadily melting, forming a new pattern, diagonally downward.

"Stairs!" exclaimed Lina. "You did it, Peter—a way down."

The glass continued to melt and mold itself, stair after stair, until a glorious staircase was complete. Joe remained standing, cage-free, on the top step, and he looked much more relaxed then moments ago. It was a beautiful sight among the ugliness to see the massive ice-like stair sculpture.

"Come on down, Joe," Peter called.

Joe looked at Peter and Lina and gave a face-swallowing smile. Peter couldn't remember ever seeing someone so happy. Joe took his first couple of steps cautiously, picking up speed as he got closer to the ground.

"Thank you, thank you," he sang as he ran toward them. He reached Peter first and held out his hand in a gesture of peace. Peter took it and shook it firmly.

"You are very welcome," Peter said nobly.

Lina was already moving toward the light under Angela's cage. "You work for me like you did for Peter," she commanded, placing her medallion in the slot as Peter had. Away it went like its twin before it, the ribbon nearly slapping Lina in the face as it fell down.

The same noises as before started from above. Lina joined Peter and Joe to watch. Soon there was another set of beautifully sculptured stairs. In a mad rush to get down, Angela tripped. The others were horrified. In the blink of an eye, the staircase molded itself into a magnificent glistening slide, catching Angela and bringing her safely to the ground. The children were astounded and cheered.

"That was kinda fun," she giggled, standing and composing herself.

They all ran up to her to greet her, and she gave a grateful thanks.

"Don't mention it," Lina said casually.

Crackling noises filled the tower, louder than the ones Lina and Peter had heard earlier. The floor beneath them began to rumble. The walls of the tower were beginning to crumble.

"Peblars!" Joe shouted.

"What?" Peter shouted back. Peter looked back at a portion of the wall. Rapidly coming out of it were figures, dark pebbled figures.

Run!

"Run!" Lina screamed.

All of the children scrambled toward the door. The dark figures continued to break themselves free of the wall. Peter had been right; he had felt something strange earlier. Joe called them Peblars, and they were watching their every move the entire time.

First out was Angela, then Lina and Joe. Peter raced desperately after the others. He took one last glance before exiting the room, and he found himself eye-to-eye with a Peblar. The moment was brief but terrifying, and Peter was not willing to stick around to see if they were friendly or not.

As soon as they were out the door, the children headed down the staircase as swiftly as possible, round and round, hoping for a gust of wind to carry them down. No such luck. The children were panting and exhausted by the time they reached the bottom. They continued toward the castle door. Joe made it to the door first and pulled hard to open it. The giant door opened a smidgen, enough to let them out. Peter was last and pulled on the handle to tug it shut. It started closing but stopped short. Long pebbled fingers were holding the door ajar. Peter let go and fled with the others.

Lina stopped, bending over to catch her breath. Joe and Angela were ahead but slowing with exhaustion. Peter ran to Lina's side, grabbing her arm and urging her forward. She fought him.

"I can't, Peter. I have no energy left and I'm having a terrible side pain." She grimaced with one hand clenching her side.

Peter looked behind them. The Peblars were still approaching. Peter thought they should have caught up by now. He noticed they seemed to move somewhat sluggishly.

"They must be weighed down by all those pebbles!" Peter said. "Please, Lina, we have to keep moving or they will catch up!"

Lina took small steps forward. "This is as fast as I can go. It hurts," she whimpered.

Joe and Angela stopped ahead when they noticed Peter and Lina were no longer accompanying them. The Peblars acted in a strange fashion.

"They've stopped," Peter stated, puzzled.

"They have?" Lina looked over her shoulder to verify for herself. "Maybe they don't want to hurt us."

Peter mulled it over, turned to face them, and called, out of breath, to the sea of pebbled faces, "What do you want with us?"

All but one of the Peblars took a step back. The one who remained was tall and quite brawny.

This gargantuan Peblar spoke, strong and bold, "All we want, dear boy, is for all of you to stay with us...forever!"

The multitude of Peblars roared with cackling-crackling laughter.

Peter was determined for that never to happen.

Joe shouted forcefully from behind him, "That is Goaltan. He is rotten, rotten to the core!"

Goaltan suddenly raised his right arm and, with great force, slammed his fist into the ground, causing the ground to split straight for Joe, stopping inches before his feet. The children's bodies trembled as they stumbled.

Goaltan laughed mightily, mimicking Joe, "Rotten, rotten to the core." His followers cheered.

Angela cried to the others, "Let's get going!"

Goaltan stomped the ground with his foot, and his followers cheered him on.

The children braced themselves, but nothing happened. They looked at one another and started to run again. Lina gained her second wind and began picking up speed, and soon the children were running side by side. Abruptly a sink hole formed beneath Lina, and she fell in, shrieking. She dangled there with one arm, nails deep in the dirt. The other children stopped immediately to help. Peter looked back and saw the Peblars starting toward them again. Urgently, the two nearest children swooped down to pull her out. Peter seized her dirt-covered hand while she swung the other one up for Joe to grab. The boys swiftly yanked her back to her feet.

The Peblars were storming closer, and Goaltan had absolute fury on his face.

"Come on, guys," Peter yelled. "We have come this far; we can do it."

The Peblars were closing in. Peter knew it would be close.

A moment later, Joe vanished. Peter smiled briefly; he knew Joe was safe. Seconds later, Angela disappeared as well. Next was Lina, but not before glancing behind her. Her eyes flashed from relief to horror before she was gone. What was the matter? Peter worried. A moment later, Peter felt warm fresh air beginning to penetrate the cold. He was going to make it; everything was going to be all right. Seconds later he could see blue-green grass, the special delivery package, and Lina's face again, and the sight comforted him. *What a lovely face.*

An ice-cold pebbled hand ripped across his chest. Peter battled the grip. He held his hand out toward Lina. She grasped it and began to pull. She could see the yellows of Goaltan's intense eyes. Joe had taken Lina by the waist to help pull. Goaltan saw this attempt and immediately started laughing, a deep disturbing laugh. Upon hearing this, the children fought even harder to free Peter.

Suddenly, Goaltan's laugh grew quieter and his face softened. Something was happening; his grip was getting warmer. Goaltan's eyes were lightening to a shade of green, and the yellows were disappearing into whites. He began rapidly losing pebbles from his body, and his grip loosened. Peter shook free easily; Goaltan was no longer trying to hold him. The children stared. His pebbled upper body was being replaced by stunning crystals.

Goaltan seemed to have forgotten about the children as he studied his arms. His laugh changed, sounding pleased.

He spoke. "At last, my old glorious self! I knew I would find Maple Town again!"

As if being pulled by force with little time to respond, Goaltan's arms and face returned to their pebbled state; he became a Peblar again. He began to laugh madly and disappeared back to his domain. What stood in Goaltan's place was the beautiful scenery of Maple Town.

The children stood for a moment in silence before Lina spoke, "Whoa, that was fun. Let's do that again!"

The others just stared at her.

"I'm kidding, I'm kidding. Seriously though, what the heck was that all about? We could have been in some serious hurt."

Angela spoke up. "You know, growing up, we were told to behave and treat others with respect and heard stories of a place like that, but that is all we thought they were: stories."

Joe added, "I used to laugh at my parents when they mentioned the stories of the Peblars. I guess I shouldn't have." Focusing his attention on Lina and Peter, he continued, "The Peblars once were

Candonites like Angela and me. Only they went terribly wrong. The most feared, the worst of the bunch, was Goaltan. We had the pleasure of meeting him. Story has it, eons ago, Goaltan was once the most beautiful Candonite anyone had ever laid eyes on. Well, you saw for yourself."

Peter interrupted, "Rock candy."

"Precisely," Joe went on. "It goes to show you that just because you are beautiful on the outside doesn't mean you are the same on the inside. He terrorized our world and wreaked pure havoc. The Candonites lived in constant fear. Something had to change. One night while Goaltan slept, ten Candonite men snuck into his home and tied him up. They carried him out and put him in a horse-drawn wagon and took him as far away as they could. The Candonites prayed and prayed that he wouldn't wake up as they traveled. When he did wake, the Candonites were already out of harm's way. When Goaltan realized what had taken place, he was so irate.

"After some time alone, he began to think it was best for him to be surrounded by the only thing he truly loved, himself. But, as the days went on, he grew bored. No one to boss around, no one to torment. He tried to come back, but he could never find home. Some say he couldn't return because the Candonites wished he wouldn't so deeply. I myself wished it just moments ago."

"So did I," said Angela.

Joe continued, "The legend goes that Goaltan looks and smells as he does now because he was so filled with hatred and so unforgiving that his heart became solid rock and the rest of him slowly turned into pebbles. He became a rotted Candonite and turned into a Peblar, nearly unrecognizable except for his stature and mannerisms. Soon after, from time to time, wretched misbehaving Candonites were said to have vanished into thin air, and a gray pebble was left in their place. Goaltan was suspected all this time. Now we know what happened to all those people."

"Peblars," Peter said. Everyone nodded in agreement.

"We just thought they were tales the elders told us to keep us in line. I certainly hadn't heard of anyone that I knew vanishing." Joe turned toward Angela. "Had you?"

"No."

"I was opening my front door to head to the parade, and when I closed it, the next thing I knew, I was in that dreadful cage. Angela was also headed to the parade. Her car door was closing and she ended up in the cage beside me."

Angela looked at Joe and back toward Peter and Lina, speaking from the heart for the both of them. "We wanted to say thank you for saving us despite the way we acted. We were real jerks, and we realize that we didn't deserve your help. If it wasn't for you two, we would have been stuck there forever and become one of them." She shivered.

Peter remembered something that sweet Mrs. Baker had said to him, and he repeated it out loud. "Mistakes are worth forgiveness if you truly mean you're sorry."

"That is why no one else had the capability to save you. *We had to forgive you.* Think of all those people who weren't forgiven," Lina became sadly aware.

All four children nodded in agreement. They truly understood.

"We really should try to get home now, Peter," Lina coaxed.

"Yeah, I'm tired of looking at your faces," Joe said, agitated.

Everyone stared at him blankly.

"Just kiddin', guys!" He laughed, and the others did, too. Lina let out a snort that made everyone laugh harder.

"Come on, let's get you two home," Joe broke the laughter.

Standing in front of the special delivery box, Peter and Lina had mixed feelings. They were happy to be going home, but sad to be leaving.

The two of them placed their hands gently on the box and took one last look at the place they had grown to love and the faces of their two new friends.

"This time, this is really it," Lina realized.

"Ready?" Peter asked her. She nodded.

Lina and Peter spoke together, "One, two,

three...free to go home!"

Peter thought he heard Angela's voice, "*Noooooo!*" from behind him, and then darkness and quickly nothing.

A Familiar Place

"Peter, Peter, wake up." He could hear Papa's voice in the distance. "Peter, it's time to go home."

"I know," he said, opening his eyes.

Papa was standing above him, his glasses nearly falling off the tip of his nose. Peter shot straight up and looked around the room for Lina.

"Where is Lina?" Peter questioned.

"What?"

"Lina, have you seen her Papa?" Peter pressed.

"Oh sure, I saw your friend earlier today. Such a nice girl. She is probably at home having dinner with her family. How are you feeling? Any better?"

"What are you talking about, Papa?"

"Oh dear, we really should get you home. I thought a nice long sleep would take care of all those sweets you ate today."

Peter felt especially guilty and he was sure it showed on his face.

"I may be an old man, Peter, but I know you snuck all those sweets you shouldn't have. Sweets are best in moderation," he said. "I believe you have learned that lesson."

"I'm sorry," Peter admitted. "Sorry for

sneaking candy I shouldn't have."

"Never mind that. Let's get you home."

"Home," Peter repeated. His mind focused back to his wondrous adventure. "I wonder if Lina made it home," he said aloud.

Papa looked at him strangely, "Of course she did, Peter."

"Papa, I looked for you earlier when I woke up and I couldn't find you anywhere. The lights were all out, the store was closed, and I didn't call home because I didn't want you to get in trouble."

"What are you talking about, Peter? I have been here all day. I closed the shop early so I could take you home now."

Peter looked at his watch. It read 4:42 p.m. "But it was 5:42 p.m. earlier, and there was this package—it was left on the table." Peter searched around for it, looking under the table. "It said 'Special Delivery' on it, and it swallowed me whole."

"Oh dear, I should have taken you home earlier."

"No, Papa, I feel fine. Ask Nana; she will know what I am talking about. She has been to Maple Town and seen the Candonites," Peter rambled.

"Nonsense, Peter, your Nana never mentioned any Candonites to me. You have been right here sleeping for quite some time. Let's get you home and straight to bed to sleep this off." Papa was adamant.

Peter was stupefied. He thought, *Could it have all been an extremely vivid dream? No, it was real...wasn't it?*

No such luck. When Papa dropped him off and told his parents what had happened, they sent Peter straight to bed. No talking to Nana and definitely no calling Lina.

Peter's father partially closed the door to his bedroom and popped his head in to say, "I know you had an interesting day, son, but try to get some rest. We love you."

They did love him, and they would listen to him if they believed a word he was saying. But it sure did seem real, every second of it.

Peter awoke the next morning feeling rejuvenated. He convinced his parents he was feeling well enough to go to school. They had no doubts when he was standing by the front door ten minutes earlier than normal, holding his lunch bag in one hand and backpack in the other. He was eager to get to school.

Peter waited around for Lina outside in the school yard. She was usually at school by now. He knew she couldn't be late to class again or she would have to stay in at recess, and he definitely did not want her to have to do that. He watched his watch count down the minutes until the first school bell rang. The students started swarming into the school, he hesitated and then joined them, looking for Lina the whole time. The second school bell rang. He was nearly to his class.

A tap on the shoulder grabbed his attention...Lina!

She took his hand and shoved something small into it. "I have to get to class!" she said frantically. He watched her rush past him, run-walking toward her own class. He was left standing in front of his. Peter opened his hand. Directly in the center of it was a piece of candy. Not any old piece of candy, but a wonderful piece of peppermint candy, complete with glued-on paper ears and tail, fishing wire whiskers, and, drawn on with permanent marker, bright blue eyes!

The final school bell rang.

Crystal Marcos has been a storyteller her entire life. Being the oldest of five children, she had a lot of entertaining to do. She is a member of SCBWI. Crystal lives on the Kitsap Peninsula in Washington State with her husband and their daughter, Kaylee. *BELLYACHE: A Delicious Tale* is her first book.

Visit her at www.CrystalMarcos.com

Made in the USA
Middletown, DE
18 February 2018